All That Remains

Not all monsters start out that way.

By Anthony J Haight

Published by Atlas & Ember Publishing™ an *AtlasUntamed* novel.

Bradford, Pennsylvania, USA
aepublishing.office@gmail.com
Visit my website!
https://ae-pub.com

ISBN: ***979-8-9991218-2-0***

Printed in the United States of America.

Dedication:

Hey Dad,

We weren't always on the same page, but I'm thankful we still had a story.

I miss you more than anything.

I still tell myself, "I'll tell him that Thursday morning."
I'm sad. I'm angry. But I'm okay.

You don't have to worry about me being sad forever — just for now.

I miss you.

Love,
Tony

P.S. I'm still the funnier one — You get it from me ;)

A Note Before You Begin:

Dear reader,

I'm sorry I don't grieve in MLA format.

I don't even grieve in straight lines.

This book is a labyrinth I built while I was falling apart.

Not neat. Not noble. Just brick after brick laid in the dark — sometimes on purpose, sometimes because I didn't know where else to put the weight.

One turn leads to *kindness.*

The next leads straight into *cruelty.*

I didn't always know which was which until I was standing there, deciding if I wanted to walk through quietly or burn it down.

Grammar frays where the feelings fray.

Sentences spill. Thoughts loop back.

Some days I pulled the walls closer to see what survived.

Some days I knocked them down just to hear the crash.

It's not a romance.

It's not redemption.

It's not a guide to living with or loving through grief.

It's not here to teach you about PTSD, gore, or the shapes violence takes. It's essentially a case study, I split my overwhelming feelings between multiple people and poked them, like you would a bruise that's begun to heal.

It's what happens when you trap grief inside a structure and force it to pace between good and evil for 300+ pages. Sometimes goodness wins. Sometimes it doesn't.

And even when it wins, it's still a loss.

This is not an autobiography.

No, I'm not Akira. Or Verath.

I don't carry a sword. I do have a tiger (adopted — save the tigers!).

I don't raise the dead.

Their relationships don't reflect my own.

I'm just an empath who feels too much at once.

It's human. That's the magic. Messy, furious, gasping-for-air human.

If you want structure, clarity, closure — that's not in here.

But if you want to feel something honest, raw, maybe a little ugly — welcome. Just… keep your hand on the wall.

It's easy to get lost in here.

This novel was written as a preservation of a storm, like a print of an oak leaf, at the time, I was trying to document and preserve my own memories from the loss. I didn't know how to exist in a world without my dad. It's not a 1:1 relation to my grief, but it's just as fluent.

—*Tony*

P.S. Now *go*—before I change my mind. :) and if you get confused, I put some info in the back of the book, consider it a cheat sheet if you will. In sections: *A Gaze of the Fallen World, Dramatis Personae (The people of Rhova), Scars in the Margins (these may vary and contain some spoilers, but may also help some, so do with it as you will.)*

Prologue

Act I: What's Left of You?

Akira, in a letter she'll never be able to send.

What's left of you?

That's all I keep asking.

Not your voice. That's already slipping from my memory. Not your laugh. I'd give anything to hear it again, but it's gone. It echoes—I know it's you—but I can no longer remember why you were laughing.
Not your body. I buried that. I carried it. Every step, every breath, I carried the weight of what he did to you. Through Calís, through Sylhalin. To the cottage we shared once.

Your friends are dead. Your past—*burned.*
Your wife and daughter, obscured in the rubble of you.
There's no one left who remembers the man, or the boy, you were before I met you.
So, what does that make you now?

When I'm the only one attending your vigil?

What's left of you, Drake?

Because gods, I'm furious.
You said everything would be alright. You said we'd make it through.
And I believed you.
You made me believe in things I'd given up on.
You smiled like it mattered.
You loved like the world hadn't ruined you yet.
And now you're just… *gone.*
Gone, and the war still isn't over. *Gone,* and the pain didn't leave with you.

I killed him. I made sure of it. I heard the last breath leave Verath's lungs.
And I thought maybe—maybe—it would be enough to stop this ache.

It wasn't.

There's a part of you still with me.
Small. Quiet. Growing.
And I don't know what to do with it.
I don't know what to do with any of this.

They'll never hear the stupid way you said my name when you were trying to make me laugh.
They'll never see how soft your eyes went when you looked at me like I was something fragile and worth holding onto anyway.
They'll never understand why I still talk to the moon some nights, like you're listening.

You deserved *more.*
You deserved *peace*. Something quiet. Something stupid and warm.
Not *me.*
You earned your fairy tale. Your happy ending. And I'm sorry you got me instead.

We deserved more than this ending.
And for that, *I'm sorry.*

So, I ask again—
What's left of you?
At the end of the world.
My world.
And I hope—somewhere—you can still hear me.
Please… take care of Theresa and Mixa.
I'll be okay.
I always am.

-Akira

Act II: What Was I Meant to Be?

Verath, the banished king, leaving Ciron behind.

Dear Mother. Dear Father.

What was I meant to be?

That's all I want to know.

Not the heir. That was never mine to claim.
Not the soldier. That was just survival dressed in *tradition.*
I was never what you wanted. Just what was left. That was clear my whole childhood. *"Go play outside, Verath."*
I wasn't the king. That came later. That came with blood. Some of it yours. *"No son of mine is going to be an alchemist. You'll enlist. Like your brothers! wipe your tears! To be vulnerable is to be weak!"* Your words reverberated through my mind even after all these years.

You told me to build something with my hands. To leave nothing behind but strength.
You told me weakness was shame, silence was failure, softness was death.

So, I *hardened.*
I *sharpened.*
I became what you wanted—or close enough that no one questioned it.

But now the ship cuts through mist, and Ciron is vanishing behind me.
The land I *bled* for. The throne I *burned* for.
Shrinking into the fog like it never knew my name.

No farewells.
No eyes on the horizon.
Just wind and silence.

I wonder if that's how it always was.
If I was ever more than a shadow in your house.
If I ever really belonged.

I carry your voices with me like a sickness. I still hear them when I hesitate. Still flinch when I breathe wrong.
Is that what you *wanted?*

All those lessons carved into my spine—did either of you ever stop to think what kind of man they'd make?
Did either of you care?
Or did you just want someone who bled better than you did?

I was the youngest.
I was supposed to follow.

But I didn't follow.
I *outlived.*
I *outlasted.*

I crowned myself king, and not one of you watched me go.

I hope wherever you are, you see what you made.
And I hope it *terrifies* you.

Because gods know it *terrifies me.*

-Verath

Part I: When the Sky Had No Scars

Chapter 1: The Ring of Justice

The birds were too loud this morning.
The wind joined them, dragging through the trees like it was looking for something.
I tied my scarf higher over my face and kept my thoughts quiet.
My katana was already in my hand, I didn't remember grabbing it.
Lolem was calling again—from beyond its gilded walls in the northeast. But I wasn't walking toward the kingdom. I was walking west, into something far older. Ectwë had begun to stir, and I was stupid enough to listen.

Count Dendrin requested I look into a job protecting Queen Cilmair of Lolem, yet again. but I'd been living a nomadic life for years.
Some say life is about settling down, having a family, living simply.
But if I'd wanted that—I would've chosen it.
I yearn for adrenaline, The thrill.
Safety doesn't feel right to me.
I stay out in the wild to stay grounded—to remember that survival is still sacred. *Hunt or be hunted.*

My boots pressed quietly through the forest. The birds had gone silent. All that remained was the sound of wind, breath, and footsteps.

I slowed my pace and took cover behind a tree. There was a band of people on the path ahead, riding in a worn-down horse-drawn cart, singing and laughing at each other. I waited until they were further away before I emerged from the shadows.

As I stepped out into the open, there was a snap from behind me. I grabbed my katana and swung it behind me, holding it to their throat. It was a man—unshaven, filthy, holding a loaded crossbow at his waist.

"Travelin' alone, are ya? Girl like you's bound to get picked up quick. Might as well pick who, eh?"

He grinned, slow and cracked.

"Didn't think I'd find dinner and a bride in the same evenin'."

His crossbow stayed down below his waist, like he thought the threat was already understood.

I kept the sword at his neck and narrowed my eyes. He's not scared. He must have friends nearby. He thinks he has a leg up, but he doesn't know—*they wouldn't be the first band of brothers I've ended.*

"What is your proposal?" I asked as I stepped closer, my boots crunching the leaves between us leaving nothing but tension.

He chuckled nervously. “Woah, hold on there. Yer’ getting a bit too close for my liking,” he said, dropping his crossbow and raising his hands.
I backed him up until his back hit a tree.
“NOW!” he shouted, in panicked yelp.

I spun and slashed my blade into his friend’s throat. The tall man grasped at it, blood gushing, dampening the weeds beneath his feet. I turned again and stopped my blade just before it severed the first man’s artery. He shrieked and whimpered.
“PLEASE DON’T KILL ME! YER SHIT ISN’T WORTH MY LIFE!”
He turned and ran, falling a few times to make sure I wasn't pursuing him.
I looked down at the cooling man at my feet—he was holding a length of chain and a dampened rag. I rummaged through his pack: a hard loaf of bread, a tome with a map of the Sarnawenian Forest, including Ectwë, and a bottle of vile-smelling liquor.
The map had a red arrow pointing to the forest’s center, with Xs over houses, clearly in the dangerous part of the forest.

A hit list? Probably abandoned homes these men ransacked and vandalized.
I closed the tome and rose. The arrow pointed south.
I wiped my blade and began heading that way.
The deeper I went, the worse the ringing in my ears became.

I heard whispers just out of reach, never in sight.
Increasing my anxiety as I entered
I finally saw houses—but no people. The sign nailed to a cracked post read Ectwë. This had once been the Heart of Magic, or so the old mystics claimed. Now it was just bones under ivy.

Something was luring me deeper, though I couldn't tell what—or why.
This part of the forest was a deep, beautiful blue hue, and the air seemed to shimmer, but it was thick—almost suffocating. My intuition kept me on course. The ancient screams continued to echo almost like they were originating in my skull.
I pulled my scarf tighter.

I stopped.

The trees had… faces? Almost as if they were painfully carved into the deep surface of the trunk, each tree's emotion burned in bright colors, each a different shade.

My steps were wary as I approached the closest tree, its face burned a firm shade of red, almost furious…?
It swung a large branch at me. It sent me flying into a stone wall of a nearby home.
My breaths hurt, the air was forcibly ripped from my lungs. Dazed, I slowly rose. My katana had already found its place in my palm, almost knowing it would lead my defensive charge.

The tree roared, a deeply rooted echo filled the rotting air surrounding us.

Its blows were slow, and easy to maneuver around. My swings cut through its branches like butter.

My dicing only made it more vengeful. Its rage only grew more insatiable. Its eyes turned a deeper shade of red.

It yanked leg like limbs out from the soil and stood nearly forty feet tall, branches and leaves falling to the ground as if it didn't need them anymore.

Sweat stung my eyes. I tightened my scarf like it could prevent the next blow.

"Bring it," I hissed.

I leapt and struck. More limbs fell to the ground, but it only grew more determined.

It wasn't about to die easy—like it had something to protect.

As I was preparing to rush forward with my katana, Its face softened, cracking and splintering into a clear face of admiration and sorrow and suddenly it knelt.

"You are carved from flint, *Little One,*" the creature rumbled. "Name yourself, warrior."

I narrowed my eyes and lowered my scarf.

"*Akira,*" I seethed softly.

I slashed into its trunk and twisted my blade, determined to end this creature for good.

It shrieked and pried my sword loose from my grip.

"I should have ended you when the earth first stirred," it bellowed, voice cracking like thunder through stone-firm silence.

It struck—I severed one hand, then the next. Then its legs.
It collapsed, sap oozing like blood.
I climbed up and held my katana to its face.
With a determined grunt of effort, I readied myself for the finishing blow.
It groaned weakly, its flame-colored features simmering softly.
I slammed my katana down; Flames ignited from inside and spread out of the husk.
The bark melted to ash.
As I plummeted to the ground, a puff of smoke cleared—and a man emerged.
I blinked, stunned as he looked at his hands like he'd never seen them before.
He approached, hand outstretched, unsure of how to greet me, I stared through him, brushed ash from my cloak, and rushed to my blade a few feet away.
No *answers*. No *explanations.* I reclaimed my katana and rushed towards him, knocking him to the ground holding him down with my boot.

Katana to his neck, the man looked up at me as fear began filling his pupils.
"WAIT–!" the man yelped.
I hesitated, my blade softly drawing blood from his neck.

I was still catching my breath, but I'd be damned if I got killed now.

As my breathing slowed, we remained still, as statues, until something in me pulled away. I yanked my katana away and proceeded to walk to the nearest house, leaving the man in the ashy remains of the creature I ended.

"HEY! WAIT UP!" he called. "What the hell just happened? What happened to Ectwë?"
I shook my head and tossed the tome and map I'd found over my shoulder, letting them drag up the dust behind me. He wouldn't find many answers in them. But maybe they'd help.
He caught up and bent to pick them up, flipping through the tome. "It was *ransacked...?*"
I shrugged softly.
He seemed stunned.
I approached the nearby house. The door was jammed. I slammed into it and crashed through, landing on the aged tiles.
He offered his hand again. I ignored it.
I didn't kill him. That was already more kindness than most got.
Rhova is collapsing in on itself, and there's no place for the nice.
Another wide-eyed fool dropped in the ruins of something that died long ago—too soft to survive, too loud to leave behind.
I didn't have time to teach him how to bleed right.
"Not much of a damsel, huh?" he asked, like he was trying to charm me.

"They said Ectwë would spit out any outsider after *The Last Resort*, Funny how it kept you."
I scoffed. "You're not the only one this place decided to *trap.*" I collapsed into the bed in the far room; I tossed my pack into the wall and closed my eyes. When I heard the man enter the room, I did my best to ignore him.

"So, you're just not going to acknowledge me? *At all?*" He asked.
I sighed and sat up, lowering my scarf.
"What do you want?" I asked in an exasperated tone.
"You're not from around here, are you?" he asked inquisitively.
I rolled my eyes. "I am from a village once in the Kingdom of Khofte. *Zodan*. It's not around anymore."
That was a lie; some of the village sank into the sea, but *some* remained.
"What do you mean not around anymore?" he asked curiously.
I sighed again and decided a half-truth was better to tell a complete stranger than my whole story.
The man slinked closer, like he was fighting the urge to bombard me with questions, he was going to want *conversation.* I fought off the sigh of annoyance at the thought.
He sat at the end of the bed as I leaned against the headboard.
It was going to be a *long* night.
I told him about how they used to talk about justice like it was a courtroom or a crown.

But in *my world?*
Justice rings loud and sharp—just before it cuts.

Chapter 2: An Ancient Flame

I sat on the floor, watching the fire grow and fight to escape the makeshift pit we made in the center of the room. My pack and sword lay beside me, a healthy distance away. The warmth of the flames brushed against my cheeks, but I didn't back away. Slowly, I unwrapped my scarf and laid it atop my blade.

The cottage was worn and weathered. The fireplace was *cracked.* The windows, *shattered.* Every gust of wind whispered through the holes in the walls like a ghost searching for a bed.
In the distance, the lights of Sarnawen flickered to the heavens, casting a golden-based aura among the stars. It looked like a promise. But through the jagged shards of glass, that promise felt *hollow*. A broken window in a broken home—if it hadn't protected its former occupants, how was it going to protect us?

"A place of refuge for those facing prosecution for magical or unearthly abilities." I said softly under my breath, I remembered the chant like an incantation, almost religiously. My mother had wished to live there once. Thinking of the phrase *almost* brought back the shimmer of magic she emanated when she spoke of the kingdom.
I sighed as I fought to ignore the surge of sadness the thought made me feel. As I turned my head back toward the man I'd found. He was a lean athletic man with tousled brown hair that I'd noticed often fell across his

forehead. His eyes, while filled with confusion, were warm, expressive and reflected wisdom and kindness, though there are shadows of old sorrows lingering in their depths. He had introduced himself as Drake the night before, his clothes were well-worn and earthy toned but effective. Now he wandered the house, mumbling strange things to himself. I observed him closely, waiting for an opportunity to grab my katana and defend myself, should the need arise.

He stood by an old bookshelf, shoulders hunched, delicately cradling something in his hands. I stepped closer and saw the worn outline of a teddy bear. Time hadn't been kind to it. His fingers trembled around the tired old fabric.

"I knew the girl who had this bear, long ago," he said quietly.
I placed a hand on his shoulder, a subtle show of sympathy. He gave a faint, grateful smile.
"Thank you," he murmured, choking back soft whimpers.

"May I ask you a few questions?" he asked with a sniffle, his tone hesitant and soft. "I know, I annoy you, but this is… a lot to process."
I gave him a small nod. His relief was obvious.
"Great," he sighed, and we sat ourselves on opposite sides of the fire.

"Why are we in Ectwë? What happened to this place?" he asked, trying to push his rising panic deep within himself, he was jittery, almost like he was trying hard not to spook me.

I shrugged. "All I know is what's considered common knowledge. The village was destroyed in search of Lord Rotik's heiress after his passing. The specifics weren't passed down."

"That's when Ectwë's elders enforced The Last Resort…" Drake chimed in.

"What's that?" I asked, steeling off my unease.

"The Last Resort was the village's last line of defense against genocide—and the extinction of mystics entirely."

I observed him closely, as the hair on my neck stood on end. He watched the flames as if they were someone close to him, bringing him comfort.

"Why were you in a tree?" I hesitated to ask. Before I knew it, the question was filling the stale air of the cottage with tension. Drake inhaled deeply and continued staring into the wilting flames.

"What was *The Last Resort?*" I asked more aggressively. My unease was quickly becoming irritation.

"*The Last Resort* was a forbidden rite passed down from the earliest tribes of my people. It's said to come from our highest deity—*Eluriah, The Keeper of Life and Flame.* The rite was said to be a merciless defense. Ultimate peace."

The flames began to falter, as if reading the room. I wasn't one to ignore divine intervention. I grabbed my katana and silently slipped outside.

The cold air was a welcome change to the warmth inside. Despite the fire's small stature, my nerves made the heat maddening. My katana rested across my back, as I crouched along the tree line. Picking through the fallen branches calmed me some.

There was some shuffling behind me. I continued gathering, my guard raised, studying my surroundings out of my peripheral vision, trying to remain oblivious.
At the next snap, I dropped the wood. The sound echoed around me. I turned, katana in hand—nothing. I searched several yards through the brush, but everything was still. I resheathed my blade and quickly stepped over the sticks and returned to the cottage.

When I stepped back into the house, Drake looked like he'd been holding his breath.
"I thought you got lost for a second, wait, where's the firewood?" he said with a nervous laugh.
I added what few sticks lie next to the pit and watched life return to the tired little flame.

Drake stared at me, lips curled slightly. His smile was… off.
"What?!" I snapped.
"Nothing…" he mumbled.

We sat in silence, crickets chirping just beyond the walls.
Then—
A crash echoed from a room nearby.

It came from the bedroom on the far side. I stomped out the fire and crept toward the wall, katana drawn. I motioned to Drake. He joined me slowly; teddy bear still in hand and reached for the doorknob.

"*Seriously? With the teddy bear?!*" I whispered sharply. He mouthed an apology and yanked open the door. Nothing. No one. The room was empty, I entered first, and Drake followed nervously. The dresser laid on the ground, various pieces of decor that were on top were shattered and broken along the floor. Drake slowly knelt down and carefully examined some of the glass shards on the floor.

I lowered my sword—but not my guard.
"Someone's watching us," I said in a firm whisper.
Drake's eyes widened as he rose, "Why would someone be watching us…?"
I shrugged. "I don't know. But they are…" I said softly.

I grabbed my pack and slid the scarf around my neck.
"Why are you gearing up? It's not even sunrise!" Drake pleaded, his voice stark with anxiety.
"We're being watched. It's not safe, we have to leave." I said, urgency thick in my voice. I left the house, heading for the road out of the village.

Drake scrambled after me. “Wait up!” he yelped.
When I reached the edge of the forest, I turned—he wasn’t there.
“Damn it,” I growled. I turned and headed back, panickily scanning for him.

A man's scream pierced the trees; I fought to follow the direction it originated.
My jog became a run as I headed deeper into the forest, branches whipping me in the face, I tried to duck and weave as I ran.

Suddenly, the forest lit up—flames roared and climbed the trees. I ducked and rolled back. Drake stood at the center of a circle of flame, hurling fire at two men attempting to put him in a person-sized cage. Panic distorted his face into something unrecognizable, his eyes burned a bright shade of red as his arms flung forward, desperate and fierce.

More figures closed in on Drake. The flames still towered over us all, licking the sky.

A man stepped through the wall of fire.

Lord Rostov.

A cruel man who hunts people for sport in the Sarnawenian forest. He never loses his prey—a formidable man.

I drew my sword and looked for a path through. I quickly climbed a tree and carefully moved branch to branch, approaching the ring of fire. I dropped down, landing with a roll and my katana drawn to Rostov's throat just as he neared Drake.

"It seems our little mystic has a warrior friend," Rostov said with a mocking smirk, raising a steady hand, his goons halted.

I stepped forward, pressing my blade deeper into his throat. His jaw clenched. Slowly, he pulled out a cigar and lit it on the edge of the blaze.

"I was just going to take the mystic. Get a thrilling hunt out of it. But I might just take you both. Really test my skills."

I said nothing, but held firm in place, I stayed between Drake and the monsters. Rostov's face lightened some.

"Feisty. I like that." He studied Drake closely. "But your friend there is a full-blooded mystic. No man holds power that long unless he is, and no one's seen one of them in a millennium." The hair on my neck stood on end, Drake?

A full blood? It's said they're the Elite of mysticism; they could do the impossible when it came to any magic.

"Take the mystic. Kill the warrior."
Rostov's cruel tone cut through the cold early morning air.

They lunged forward. I fought them off. Blade met blade. The first one dropped to his knees—headless. Another, throat slit. The rest? Persistent. An endless swarm of men it seemed.

Drake staggered. His fire faltered, he seemed woozy.

"I don't… I…" his voice was hollow as he wavered.
He collapsed just behind me. "NO! DAMN IT!" I screamed.

More of them closed in. I struck again desperate—another fell. A blade sliced my left cheek. Blood ran hot, I barely felt it, but it enraged me further.

I snarled, swinging harder, pushing one man back with a kick to the ribs. He met my blade with his.
"You're surrounded! Give up!" he shouted manically.

Wrong move.

I surged forward, found my opening, and drove my katana through his throat and into the tree behind him. His eyes went wide as I watched his essence dampen my katana. I yanked my blade free and heard a scuffle behind me.

I turned—*too late.*

Rostov had locked Drake in the cage and climbed into the wagon.

“HEY!” I screamed.

The horses burst forward. I ran as fast as I could, my legs burned as I tried to catch the wagon. I was fast. just not fast enough.

I dropped to my knees, my chest heaving. They were gone.

Damn it.

I pressed my forehead to the dirt, fists clenched.

Rage. Panic. Shame. Exhaustion. The emotions were all too familiar to me.

How could I have let this happen? *again?...*

For years I’d kept my guard up. Never let anyone in. Now, in one stupid night, I slipped—and it cost someone else everything. *again…*

My first real human connection in months… *gone.*

All I could do was watch.

I swore I'd never feel this *helpless again.*

Not after *her.*

But the ache wouldn't leave.

Chapter 3: The Hunt

A dense, silvery fog hung over the morning as I crept along the forest's edge, boots silent in the dew-soaked grass. Each step carried the memory of recent failures—Drake lost to Rostov, the echo of the cage lock clashing closed. I'd replayed it again and again, guilt knotting tight in my chest. The urge to fix things burned inside me, transforming shame into a fierce protectiveness—I would not let myself fail those who depended on me, not again.

I moved with purpose, each step softly navigating thorn and root, my heart hammering with an odd mix of hope and dread. The air, a cold mix of anxiety and early morning dew, Rostov's camp loomed ahead: I've been observing them for a few days, cages filled the clearing, and a crumbling castle bordered the far side of the camp. Some cages were empty, Rostov has been busy the past couple days, the remaining containing the unlucky. I crouched behind a felled log, eyes scanning for movement. The muffled cries of prisoners filtered through the air. Inside one cage, Drake sat slumped, face bruised but defiant. In another, a tiger cub—a flash of gold and white, ears pinned back in fear. Rostov freed an older one, *the cub's mother* was my best guess. from that cage yesterday evening. My heart ached for the poor creature, …all *alone*, and afraid of its own solitude. Tigers are almost extinct. The thought of Rostov hunting it made my mouth sour.

I edged closer. One guard patrolled the cages, spear resting on his shoulder. I slipped through the brush, patience holding me back until he stopped to yawn and to peer into the trees. My katana flashed—swift, silent, final. He crumpled to the ground, barely a sound. I didn't stop to think about it. No time. No hesitation. Just one less threat between me and the man I have sworn to protect.

I raced to the cages, heart pounding.

"*Akira—*" Drake's voice was hoarse, but relief lit his eyes. He's *alive*. I told myself that was all that mattered—but something in me *surged*. I shoved it down.
"Quiet," I hissed, kneeling by the lock. I drew a small pouch from my belt, picking at the crude mechanism until it clicked open.
"*Stay* behind me." I swung the gate open. Drake stumbled out, wincing but steady. I hesitated as we turned to leave, a trembling whimper from the cub *creeped* down my spine, His mother is *gone*. Rostov will make sure he's next. Before I knew it, I had quickly darted to the cub's cage next. "*Where are–?*" Drake began to ask "Shh," I said softly, the little creature shrank back into a small pile of bones, but I murmured gentle words and held out my hand. It hesitated, but then desperately pressed its nose to my palm. The warmth of its breath surprised me—fragile but still fighting to survive. "That's it, *cutie*." I murmured softly. The cub yowled quietly as I attempted to grab it.

The sound of footsteps—more guards approaching. I shoved the cage open wider, scooped up the cub, and pressed it into Drake's arms.
"*Run.*" I ordered.

We fled into the forest. Branches whipped my arms; behind me, shouts rang out. My mind raced: *keep them moving, don't let them get cornered.* For a moment, the world narrowed to the pounding of my feet, the cub's wild whining under Drake's hands, the fear that we *might not* make it. But the trees closed around us, hiding our trail, and the shouting faded to the eerie quiet of the forest surrounding our quickened panting.

The world didn't stop chasing us. But for a few moments, we were *faster.*
We ran until we couldn't hear the camp at all. I collapsed beside a mossy boulder, gasping for breath. Drake sat next to me, the cub in his lap—wide-eyed, trembling, but alive. "I can't believe we just did that…" Drake said, "WE *ESCAPED!* THANK YOU, AKIRA!" Drake was ecstatic. He tried to pull me into a hug, but I firmly stood up. "*Shhh!* you want us *all* in a cage this time?" I said angrily. Drake gave me a long blink, and his face shrunk from embarrassment. "*Sorry…*" he whispered. As I stood above them, my heart sputtered in my chest as I looked at them: battered, but free. That guilt gave way to something *softer*, something fierce and protective. I would never let them be taken again. Whatever else happened, I would keep these two safe—even if it meant losing myself.

For the first time in days, I let myself hope. Maybe we'll be *okay*.

Chapter 4: The King of Ciron

Act I: Where Power Begins to Rot

I hadn't seen land for four months, and I wasn't sure whether I wanted to *conquer* it or *burn* it to ashes.

I stood at the edge of the *White Mist*, the ship groaning beneath my boots as the sea hissed around us. After four months at sea, the port of Eîthor finally crept into view—a grey crown on the continent's jagged brow.

Beyond it, my fortress rose like a threat. The *last* outpost under my banner. In a valley that struggled with farmland, and population, the towering cliffsides shadowed most of the kingdom,

And unfortunately, the *only* way out of the valley was through *Sylhalin*.

Eîthor mostly survived on fish and imported food from Ciron every four months, the last place I held in the *Land of Light* that hadn't fallen.

Ciron and Rhova—two continents at war for far longer than memory serves. The Light called it order. The Dark called it freedom. Neither side understood mercy.

The captain barked, “DISEMBARK FOR EÎTHOR LIBERTY, LADS!”

Sailors scattered with whoops and cheers, their boots clapping against the gangplank. I kept my hood up, cloak drawn tight, and let them pass me by.

The legends say the White Mist earned its name from the fog that gathers after the worst storms—storms it survives *untouched. Untouchable*, like its captain claims.

I stepped onto solid ground and didn’t flinch. But the ache in my knees reminded me I’d been at sea too long. I’d grown used to the sway—now everything felt *too* still.

Whispers coiled around me like smoke.

“*He shouldn’t be here.*”
“*He’s losing the war—what’s he doing here?*”
The voices persisted as I pulled my hood lower to obscure my face.
I walked on.

The front tower of my fortress loomed higher with each step from the dock. As I approached the gates, a guard moved to block me.

“This area is off-limits, sir—” His voice caught in his throat as recognition set in. He straightened instantly. “M-my apologies, my lord.”

I entered the keep. Soldiers stiffened. Whispers followed me through stone halls. They looked at me like a ghost haunting its former home. Like something they thought they'd buried years ago.

"*He came back...?*"
"*W-why...?*"

Once, those voices *would've* cheered.

I strode to the terrace and raised my voice. "If any of you doubt our cause—*step forward.*"

Six men broke formation, nervous eyes darting to each other.

"Excellent," I said. "Follow me to the throne room."

They obeyed, silence weighing down each step as I led them into the throne room. "Kneel," I commanded. They did. I drew one of their swords from its scabbard.

I pointed the blade at the first soldier.

"Name," I asked firmly.

He swallowed. "Captain Renner, sir."

Renner. He used to carry my banner. Held the line at Ruen's crossing.

"Do you have doubts, Captain?"

A pause. "If I may speak freely—we're outnumbered. The Pillars hold five regions. We hold one."

I nodded once. "And I rule an *entire* continent, Ciron stands ready for my command."

Before he could reply, I swung the sword. His head hit the floor before his body.

My hands didn't shake.

The others stared, *frozen*. One of them broke—eyes wide, shoulders trembling, fear spilling out in quiet whimpers.

"Anyone else?" I asked, my voice light. *Too light.* "Critique my swing, perhaps? *Too low*?"

I grinned faintly, but it didn't reach my eyes. One of them started to cry.

"*My gods,*" I muttered. "Get out. I can't even look at you."

They scrambled to obey, dragging his corpse like a broken piece of furniture.

I returned to the terrace.

“The Pillars believe they can rewrite the balance of the world,” I called out. “But Light and Dark *must* coexist—or destroy each other trying.” People began to crowd together in the courtyard.

A steward rushed forward, breathless. “My lord—Eîthor is under siege. Lord Esíos advanced early. He knows you’ve returned.”

Of course he does. Wolves *always* smell blood first.

I nodded. “Then we hold.”

Orders poured from my mouth like steel: archers to the walls, to the medical tents, knights to the gate. The outer districts would fend for themselves. We’d protect the core.

And then—across the horizon—soldiers. Columns of them. A man on horseback broke formation and rode forward.

“*VERATH!*” he echoed.
I stepped onto the edge of the terrace, cloak snapping in the wind.
And I leaped.

Act II: Victory Wears a Mourning Veil

"*VERATH!*" Esíos screamed from outside the wall.

I landed on a rooftop with a roll, traveling quickly across the tiles until I reached the overlook above the gate. The valley beyond the fortress teemed with Esíos' soldiers, their formation a dark tide beneath the late morning mist.

"Wow. It's an honor to meet the great Banished King of Ciron in person!" Esíos called, spreading his arms theatrically. "We heard you were coming home today, so we came to offer the *warmest welcome*. And what's warmer than blood pouring from your soldiers' chests?"

He laughed and rattled his sword between the slats of the gate. "We're here to ask for a peaceful surrender. And we'll even say *'plea—'*"

"I'm afraid we'll have to decline," I said, cutting him off before he could finish.

Esíos froze.

His smile died and his breath caught—

"YOU INTERRUPT ME?!" he roared, voice cracking like thunder against the stone. He threw his helmet to the ground with a metallic shriek. "I come here—I come *here*—offering you mercy, and you *DARE* cut me off like some petty barmaid?!"

His horse reared from the sheer heat of his rage.

"You think this is a game?" he shouted, spinning to his troops like they might join in the madness. "He thinks he's better than us! –*Thinks* he can just say no!"

He turned back, shaking with fury. "You're not *noble*. You're not *brave*. You're a dead man, Verath. A corpse screaming fancy words!"

I nodded slowly. "Because they're not fighting for me. They're fighting for freedom."

I slid my hand behind my back and gripped my dagger. A woman nearby caught my signal. She nodded, passed it along the wall.

"You go for him," she said softly. "We've got your back, sir."

Esíos turned his back, and I moved. I leapt from the wall, dagger in hand. The steel punched into his shoulder. He shrieked and flung me off as chaos exploded around us.

Arrows rained from the walls. Archers took down horses. Knights clashed at the gate. Clerics rushed to the wounded.

My dagger remained buried in Esíos' flesh.

"HE'S *MINE*!" he bellowed at his men as I rose to my feet and armed myself with a fallen sword.

He charged like a bull. Our blades clashed hard—once, twice, again. I blocked the third with a twist and jabbed for his ribs, but he spun away.

"You think you can take me?!" he roared. "I was chosen to defend *Sylhalin*—the Gated Kingdom itself! I am *unstoppable!*"

He struck low and fast. I parried—*barely*—but the force still rattled my arms.

"*Hold on!*" the woman from before shouted from behind me. She was weaving through the melee, dodging blows to reach us.

"*Distract* him—I'll find an opening!" I shouted back.

She nodded, fear in her eyes. She wasn't ready, but she came anyway.

Esíos bared his teeth in a snarl. "She won't save you, *Verath!* You're brittle! That's why the Lord *hates* you—because weak men like you make other fools think they have a chance!"

He lunged. I ducked, swept his legs, and slashed. He blocked in time but stumbled.

The woman leapt with a cry, aiming for his throat. Her blade *would've* ended it—if his neck hadn't turned to silver after impact.

Her sword bounced off. She hit the ground, rolled, and raised her shield.

"*WHAT ARE YOU?!*" she screamed.

Esíos cackled. "I am the bane of your existence!"

He struck her shield with brutal force. Again. Again. She was gasping, barely holding.

I moved quickly trying to interrupt his flurry of blows. I saw his back turn. I ran, blade low, steady. One step. Two.

I thrust my blade into his back.

Steel drove through his spine and out his chest. He froze. He choked and sputtered blood.

"*But—how?*" he whispered.

"You talked too much," I said firmly over his shoulder.

Blood spilled from his lips. His sword slipped from his grasp.

He dropped to his knees.

"You *won't* win," he muttered. "They'll send better than me. Ones who don't flinch. Ones who don't care. The Lord doesn't fear you—he just hasn't used you yet."

The female soldier stepped beside me, chest heaving.

"You said we'd lose this fight too," she muttered.

He tried to speak again. But the breath left him. His body slumped forward.

She spit on his corpse. "*Asshole*." Then she kicked him for good measure. "Sick of this bastard."

She turned to me, wiping her blade clean. "*What the hell* was that trick? His skin—it turned to *metal*."

I stared down at the body, the gleam of silver fading like breath on glass.

"I've seen it before. Years ago, during the Frost Rebellion in Ciron." My voice lowered. "A warlock named *Xavien the Undying.* Same magic. His skin turned to silver when we struck him. Blades bounced off like paper darts. We lost dozens trying to bring him down."

Her eyes widened. "And you did?"

"We thought we did," I said. "But they called him the *Undying* for a reason."

She moved to tend the wounded. I called the nearest soldier and ordered scouts to the outer wall and the portside district.

The valley was a grave. My cloak, dark blue as night's stark embrace dragged through blood and broken stone.

Next was Sylhalin.

I turned to my army. Raised my blade.
"SYLHALIN WILL FALL!" I roared.They echoed back, fire in their voices. "We strike at sunrise," I said under my breath. *"They'll never see it coming."*

Chapter 5: The Rightful Queen

I stood on the balcony near the peak of my castle and watched as the sun began to set on the blackened bricks of my refuge, hope evaporating in real time with the light. My soldiers dragged bodies—*friend and foe*—and threw them into piles outside the walls, billows of black smoke barreled upward. I couldn't help but have a sense of anxiety as I watched the years, I'd had poured into this place slowly burn and rise to the sky… my focus turned to my hands, I could feel the sweat coating them, making them slick. I wiped them on my shirt, which helped the sweat but not the numbness in my digits. I have reluctantly accepted what I've been told: a siege on Sylhalin has to wait until my citizens grieve their loved ones. My hope is that we may continue with my plan soon.

"*Sir…?*" a shy man approached and spoke from behind me. I turned. My cloak fluttered behind me with a *whoosh.*

"What is it?" I asked softly, trying to mask my anxiety as irritation.

He looked at me with a frown and referenced a tome he had in his grasp. "I've tallied our casualties. I figured we could hold a memorial service for the fallen. The masses would be more comfortable—and confident in our cause—if we show some sympathy and support for the dead. Morale is *dangerously* low, sire," he explained.

"*Morale*. An excuse for layman folk to slack on their duties, Verath, sympathy won't help you in your war." I could hear my father's disapproval echoing in my bones as a chill ran down my spine. I let out a shaky exhale as I reoriented myself.

"Would you like to have an official service?" he asked. His voice cracked and rose an octave as he finished.

"*Sure*. Starting tonight. Have families say a few things, and I would like to clear tomorrow and give them a moment to grieve—*but no more than that.* War waits for no one," I said with a quick nod and turned away from the man and retreated back towards the balcony.

"Yes, sire." He gave a light bow, and I heard the door close with a low slam.

I stood there, watching the view, before adjourning to my quarters.

I sat at a desk in my chambers, staring at a map of Rhova where I had drawn my last excursion here. I looked over each kingdom and realized—it was outdated. Several alliances weren't current anymore. I hadn't been here since the First Age, when my father held this refuge. I was just a low-level leader. Following his orders like the rest.

I stood up from my desk, exited my room into the corridor, and ventured downstairs in search of a servant. I eventually encountered one in the main hall.

"You there! I'm in need of your assistance," I stated firmly.

"How may I be of service, my lord?" he asked.

"I need you to get me a cartographer and a scout or two. I need to create a current map of the continent—each kingdom and village."

He nodded. "I will fetch them for you, my liege." He bowed and walked away.

I turned and began to head back toward my quarters. "Who am I kidding? I won't be able to sleep. Too much to do," I mumbled. "Best make my way to the library. Maybe I can find some information on the more recent history of the Pillars."

I walked into the library with sky-high ceilings and dark oak bookshelves filling each wall. The one vacant wall had a large stained-glass window filled with various colors creating a mosaic of a beautiful landscape of Calís. I began searching the shelves. I found four tomes that might be useful. I moved to the large table in the center of the room and began reading.

In the third tome, I found that early in the Second Age, all the Kingdoms of Light had been conquered by a lone soldier named Rotik. He entered each kingdom and slaughtered all the royals until only he remained. He ruled not only his own kingdom, but the other four.

Eîthor was the only one he ignored—not because it posed a threat, but because he believed it would fall on its own. It just never did.

Rotik not only became king of all Pillars—he also had two heirs. When Rotik passed, his sons killed each other in a duel for the throne. It's also told that he had a child—*a baby girl*—with a woman from Ectwë.

Ectwë was a mystic-based village. All its citizens were well-versed in magical powers and potions. With no remaining heirs, a group of knights ventured to find the king's remaining child, but to no avail. They never found her, so they appointed a Lord until Rotik's heiress emerged. She never did.

There were false claims, but none possessed powers resembling the child's mother. It's said she had the ability to manipulate plant life on a massive scale—unheard of, as most magic was linked to other elements or healing.

She refused to reveal where her child was, and as a result, she was tortured to death.

"*My god...*" I gasped. *"Enough! Don't show emotion, Verath."* I shook my head furiously as if his voice would fall out, it never did.

"Sir, your guests have arrived. Shall I bring them up?" the servant asked.

"Yes, thank you," I replied. The servant nodded and disappeared.

A few minutes later, two men entered along with the servant. The servant pointed to the table and left. The men sat down—one to my left, the other to my right.

"You requested a map?" the man on the left asked.

"Yes." I explained the complexities I was looking for. He nodded, and the scout added information about each region and kingdom. I took a few moments to ask about the information I'd found in the third tome.

The scout explained, "The Lord they appointed in the Second Age is still in charge—Lord Roldan. Some say that Rotik's long-lost heiress is still alive, living in one of the six kingdoms. But that's pure speculation. No one knows for sure. After the village of Ectwë was destroyed in a long battle, all mortals who entered were slaughtered. The mystics' numbers dwindled. More and more of them retreated to other kingdoms and began living in hiding."

"It's been so long, anyone you meet might have powers. Many mystics reproduced and boosted their population, some groups *vanished* entirely, no one knows why, but it's not even an elven gene anymore—"

"Anyone of any race can possess power, as long as one of their parents had them," he explained.

I nodded and tried to retain the information. "Rotik's bastard may emerge in the battles to come—and could challenge any of the current sitting royals for their throne. She *could* be an asset, if you can find her." Father's voice seemed to echo with menacing glee.

"How *could* we find the heiress?" I asked the scout.

"…*Maybe.* But it's highly unlikely. People have been looking for decades. She's got to be in her late thirties—living in plain sight, or maybe she died long ago. But either way… what makes you think we should even attempt it?" he asked.

"*GODS!* Just when I thought you had some useful followers, turns out they are just as inept as my son!" Father's voice bellowed, filling all the space in my ears.

"I didn't ask your opinion. I was inquiring on how you'd start looking," I snapped angrily.

I slammed my fist into the table. The cartographer jumped. The scout commander visibly tensed. I felt nothing but the aching sting of my father's guidance. "*Good. They're listening now.*" Father said calmly.

The cartographer continued scribbling, trying not to make eye contact with me. Deep down, I understood why I had to be this way, but part of me felt wrong… almost sad for being so frightening. He was already at the third Pillar—Sarnawen—and sketching major points of interest.

The scout commander cleared his throat nervously. "We'd start in the Forest around Ectwë. Where her mother was from. And slowly work our way around the countryside up to Sarnawen."

"Then that's where we'll start. Form a party, but do not attempt to leave yet. We cannot pass through the Gated Kingdom across the valley—we'll be slaughtered. First, we conquer it. Then we may venture out," I ordered.

"Yes, sir." He left as quickly as he arrived.

The cartographer was nearly finished with the updated map. He'd captured all Light Pillars, the rivers, and the stone mountain barriers that separated Eîthor from the rest of Rhova.

I asked him to find me when he was finished. He nodded, and the scout offered to help him with finishing touches.

I headed to the terrace and observed the inner wall closely—soldiers training, talking, marching. Beyond the wall, *life continued*. Civilians watched as the corpse fires burned low.

I inhaled deeply and kept watching, the warm moonlight soothing the onslaught of emotions rattling around in my skull. I turned and was faced with my father's translucent green figure blocking my reentry to the keep. "Move." I ordered, with a shaky exhale. "*Ha.* Don't pull the fake authority with me *Verath,* if I can see through it so can everybody else, Esíos saw it, everybody else you encounter will see it and *know*. You aren't worth the title of king. Your mother knew it; your brothers knew it. *I know it. Banished,* is the only way anyone sees you." he approached as he spoke— each step darker, the translucent green slowly blooming with a tinge of red. "*You disgust me, Verath.*" he vanished without another word. I fell to my knees and let out a deep sob, I hadn't realized I had been holding my breath that whole time. I collapsed to the floor of the terrace, staring at the moon, *heartbroken*, *furious*, and *disappointed* in myself as well, but unlike my father, I knew I could do this, I am worthy.

My hopes had slowly returned. *Tomorrow*…we just may be able to attack the Gated Kingdom—and we'll carry in Esíos' head… on a pikestaff.

Chapter 6: The Cleansing plague

Act I: Ashes in Waiting

I sat in the war room I had convened, hoping to gather enough intelligent minds to create a salvageable plan to conquer the Gated Kingdom of Sylhalin. Unfortunately, we were just as unprepared as before. Already behind my schedule and blocked by sheer geography—no one could enter the kingdom from Eîthor. It was the only way out of the valley.

Some soldiers had suggested mobilizing our best support to take the gates by force, but we lacked the numbers for a siege of that scale.

I watched the sunrise filter through the stained glass. Red light passed over the black marble table, igniting thoughts I hadn't voiced aloud. Flames outside mirrored the idea.

"What if we attack with flame troops in front? Their gates are wooden—we'd breach them easily. The houses and walls are marble, yes, but the entry point would be ours," I finally suggested. "Another dumb idea from my dumbest child." Father said with venom, I rolled my eyes and ignored him.

A scout nodded. “It’s not the worst idea. They’ll have archers on the walls. If we can burn the gate before getting into their range, we might cut our losses.”

“I like him, he understands you're only as strong as your army, and you, Verath, aren't.” I fought to maintain composure, like his words didn't hurt.

A few hours later, a cleric entered quietly. She closed the door and kept to the wall.

“Sir, I have an urgent matter I’d prefer to discuss in private,” she whispered.

I excused myself from the group and led her into my study. “What is it?” I asked.

She pulled down her kerchief, her hands trembling. “There’s an illness spreading in the port district. High fevers, chills… but worse—rashes so severe that skin peels with a touch. The doctors are overwhelmed. Some of the sick collapsed in the streets. If this continues, we’ll face mass panic.”

I studied her face. Fear radiated from her like heat. She was young, maybe mid-twenties, but she wore exhaustion like armor.

“Thank you for bringing this to my attention, Ilyse.” she had been giving updates since day one. “Separate the infected and the corpses. Move them to the far end of the valley. Do it discreetly, if you can."

"Yes, sir." She replaced her kerchief and vanished like mist.

I hung my cloak and returned to the war room.

"My apologies. What did I miss?" I asked.

"Nothing yet," someone muttered. "Same stalemate."

"What was that about?" a scout asked.

"There's a plague spreading in the port. Symptoms include high fever, chills, and skin that peels like burned parchment." I sat at the head of the table. "The clerics are struggling. It's worsening fast." I stated.

The room fell quiet—except for two scouts still poring over maps.

"You're unmoved by the dying?" Thalia snapped at them. Her name had only recently made its way to my attention, but her presence already felt like a gale in a still room. "Tear your eyes off those lines and join us in reality!" she squawked.

She snatched papers from the table and flung them. They scattered like feathers, sharp with tension.

One scout stood, jaw clenched. “We’re here to plan a war, not wring our hands in prayer.”

“And we’ll lose that war,” she shot back, “if half our soldiers are rotting from the inside out!”

“We don’t even have a way to reach Sylhalin with their gates and cliffs—” the scout yelled.

“Then we’ll find a way to even the scales,” she hissed.

Another scout leaned forward, slowly grinning. “Even the scales… yes. Yes! We just need an engineer. Someone who helped build the aqueduct system!”

“What would they build?” she asked, her voice brittle.

He didn’t answer. Instead, he walked her to the window. We all turned.

Outside, clerics wheeled the dead through the streets. Families screamed and clung to one another. Some corpses burned in distant piles. Others—too many—waited in silence.

The scout whispered, “We’ll use the corpses as weapons.”

Thalia gasped, hands over her mouth.

I didn't flinch. Not because it didn't repulse me—but because I couldn't afford the luxury of hesitation.

"Indeed," he said. "We just need a method to get them over the cliffs. That's what the engineer is for."

"Only then," I muttered, "will the Gated Kingdom fall."

And we all stood in that room—half of us disgusted, half calculating—while a plague became a plan.

Act II: Fire Is the Cure

Fevers. Chills. Raw skin. I was finally seeing firsthand the illness spreading among my people.

Ilyse assured me that a simple facial covering would help prevent infection.

The coughing, the sobbing—the air felt thick, almost heavy, as if something waited.

I pulled my focus from the masses and turned toward the makeshift graveyard facing Sylhalin.

I walked down the rows of infected corpse piles and watched the flames destroy everything that once was a person.

“My lord! This way!” a woman shouted with an anxious wave.

I looked back at the flames and finally walked toward her. As I approached, she gave me a bow and nodded for me to follow.

“Virmath wanted me to fetch you. He has something to show you!” she said with an excited squeal. She had the highest spirits of anyone these past few days.

She pointed to a wooden machine ahead of us.

The closer we got, the harder it was to decipher.

"Ah, the King himself. Greetings, my lord," the scruffy dark elven man said with a bow.

I lowered my face covering and nodded to him.

"Where are my manners? Excuse my disrespect, sire. I'm Virmath. I'm a sailor by heart, but I'm not bad with my hands, as you can see." He patted the wheel of his wooden machine.

"I was told to make something to help with transporting large items quickly—like projectiles," he said with a smile. "My starting contraption took something after a crossbow, but it wasn't functional. But this baby is a completely different concept. Same idea. To start, we put our item here—" he approached the giant net at the back, "—then we position it, and finally we cut this rope here, and…"

He sliced the rope with his blade. A bundle of corpses flew into the cliff face faster than anything I'd ever seen. I gave a wicked smile beneath my kerchief.

"Voilà! That was just a test run. Obviously, we'd need an actual target next time. But I think this is just the thing you need to get something over them walls. Not to mention, they're a pain to reload—so multiple shots are unlikely—but I can try to make more." Virmath stopped and took a deep breath, like he hadn't breathed since he started talking.

"Is that a small smile I, see? I assume you like my do-hickey?" Virmath chuckled.

I nodded. "It is quite impressive. You turned an impossible thought into a tangible machine. I'm impressed." I gave him a light smile and extended my hand. He shook it with glee.

"It's an honor, sir," he said.

I nodded. "I'm sure it is. I'd like you to meet with the group I've assembled. We'll be meeting in an hour—you could add quite a bit to the discussion."

"Of course." He gave me a wave as I turned back toward the worn-down grass paths leading into town.

Just as I was about to turn toward the castle gate, a woman grabbed me and screamed.

"HOW CAN YOU LET US LIVE LIKE THIS?! IT'S INHUMANE!" she sobbed.
"Ignore her Verath, such stupidity doesn't merit a response." Father echoed.

I was speechless. I had no response to her pleas. I just continued on my way and left her wailing in the road, my heart sunk as a breath got stuck in my throat. I stood tall trying to remain the commander I had to be.

The guards opened the portcullis with a loud, rusty squeak.

An hour had passed since I ventured outside the inner wall into the valley.

I stood at the window and watched the valley fires dwindle down. It had been five days since the battle with Esíos, and yet it seemed like attacking Sylhalin was still far from my grasp.

I was eager to get it done and over with already, maybe the tingling in my hands and feet would recede.

There was a rapid knock at the door.

I turned from the window and faced it. “Enter.”

Virmath smiled as he entered. “Am I early?” he asked, glancing around the empty room.

“No. The group is in the room across the hall,” I explained. “I’m actually glad you’re here. I’d like to talk to you privately before we join the group.”

He nodded and sat in the chair across from my desk.

"I'd like to know how long it would take you to make more of that machine of yours," I asked.

He looked around my study, then finally opened his mouth. "That prototype took me a day—but I worked straight through. If I had help, I could get more finished quicker," he said warily.

"Fantastic!" I said gladly. "I want you to get to work as soon as possible. We're already behind schedule. If we can take down the gates and some of the soldiers beyond the wall, we could invade in a matter of hours."

I smiled. Finally—some good news. Sylhalin will fall tonight, whether we're prepared or not.

I could feel the anticipation in my fingers.

I led Virmath into the conference room. The group turned their attention to him as I introduced him. They exchanged pleasantries.

Virmath explained that he needed help building more machines. The exact words he used were "flinger-machines." The group agreed to assist.

I spoke from the end of the table. "Finish before morning. I'd like to ambush Sylhalin before the night passes."

I left the room, the group still processing the sudden deadline.

I walked into the courtyard and started informing my captains about what was happening.

"Tonight? You want me to have my men ready for battle tonight…?" the captain asked in surprise.

I nodded lightly.

He chuckled and sighed. "Fine. I don't agree with this—but I'll spread the word."

In a matter of thirty minutes, even the townspeople had begun building Virmath's machines. I had no idea how Virmath convinced them to halt their sobbing and help. We had knights training with swords and shields. Clerics preparing their medicines and spells. Everyone seemed to have a role.

I walked to my study, put on my cloak, and looked into the shattered, aged mirror.

I took a deep breath and opened my eyes to see my reflection had vanished from view.

"Good to see I'm not rusty." It wasn't just a parlor trick. At its weakest, the flickering power allowed me to vanish from sight—from mirrors, from still water, even from the eyes of those who looked directly at me. In that silence, I walked among the spirits, unseen and barely felt.

I took another breath. My reflection returned.

I grabbed my dagger and headed to the courtyard.

Just as I exited the castle, a horn sounded in the distance.

I flipped up my hood, drew my dagger, and moved to cover behind the barracks. I didn't see anything unusual—but I heard something. Chanting?

I stuck to the shadows and moved closer.

It wasn't chanting— was it synchronized footsteps?

Were Imperial soldiers marching toward the gate?

I looked around, but my followers had vanished.

I grabbed a bow and quiver from the barracks and headed to the roof for a vantage point.

I searched the surrounding area but didn't see any enemy troops.

A loud *squeak* echoed in the still evening air.

In the distance, the top of the wall bordering Sylhalin and Eîthor clanked to life and began to move. A giant cage erupted from the wall around the city streets nearest the gate, connecting to its opposite sides—forming a protective dome over the distant city.

"*What the hell…?*" I whispered in disbelief. I had never seen such a marvel in technology as grand as it before.

The marching grew louder. *Were they in the keep?*

"*Shit… shit… shit…*" I muttered.

I took a deep breath, stepped onto the ledge, and *jumped*—aiming for the alchemist's shop below.

I landed with a roll and ran for the gate.

I *had* to find out what was going on. I ran for the portcullis of my refuge and found it raised, in the distance I found my citizens, enraged, tired of waiting, of excuses from me, dealing with those responsible for their ache directly. I ran as fast as I could, but the horde begun flinging flaming corpses, rays of flame streaked the starry night skies.

As I finally approached the Sylhalin gates, I found a mob of my followers *fighting, screaming.* I drew my blade and charged into the fray.

A woman bumped into me. "Oh, sorry," she mumbled. She turned to see my face and bowed. "My *lord*. Glad to make your acquaintance once again." she launched an arrow at a guard beyond the wooden slatted gates as we spoke.

I *recognized* her. She'd *helped* me in the battle with Esíos. I may not be standing if not for her.

"What's your name?" I asked.

She tilted her head. "*Now you want to exchange pleasantries?!* I'm Laurel!" she shouted over the chaos.

Something was *different* about her. I couldn't place it.

Before I could ask more, she vanished into the crowd.

Was it *her* that was different? Or *me*?

The Imperials had posted archers above us, thinning the herd at the gates. But my soldiers were prepared—taking down archers and shielding civilians.

The wooden gates began to crumble.

"FIRE!!" a man screamed from behind me.

It was Virmath—leading the charge.

Burning corpses soared into the gates. Net-bound ones flung over the wall into the slats of the iron-bar dome, raining into the city despite the defense.

The gates burned and collapsed in on themselves.

The mob stormed the streets—Sylhalin soldiers and civilians alike, falling to the fury of my people.

Fires lit the buildings. White streets filled with blood.

As I finished off a soldier, someone pulled me into an alley.

"Shhh," a shadowed man whispered, waving me deeper in.

We reached a dead end lit by a torch.

He was a light-skinned high elf. Short hair. Light green eyes. Medium height. His ears pointed up—unlike the dark elves of Eîthor.

"We would like to help," he said.

I looked around and saw no one else.

"Who? … I just see you," I said cautiously.

He sighed—and whistled.

Elves dropped from rooftops, filling the alley.

“These are the people of Sylhalin,” he said confidently, “and we’d like to join your cause.”

Chapter 7: They Didn't Call Me a Monster—Yet

Act I: What He Saw Beneath the Hood

The light elf leader snapped, and the crowd of elves disappeared into the darkness in an instant.
He then turned to the brick wall behind him and whistled a peculiar tune—it was hard to hear over the sounds of battle just outside the alley.
The wall rumbled, and the bricks moved as if by magic to reveal a stairway going down into an underground… something.
The elf nodded towards the tunnel and began descending the stairs.

I reached for my dagger and followed. I was suspicious of him, but he had ample opportunity to kill me—and didn't.
"Where are we going?" I asked sternly, trying to avoid sounding like prey.

A nearby torch burst into flame with a whoosh. More followed, both sides of the tunnel lighting up by a series of torches.
"We Sylhalinians have been tortured, enslaved, and forced into the imperial armies.
Families were separated—women, children, even infants taken from their mothers.
The last of us have resorted to an underground defensive approach."

I listened to his concerns. It seemed he had a bone to pick with the Imperials, so he could be a useful ally.

"I know you have no reason to trust me or my fellow elves, but your assault on Sylhalin has granted us the perfect opportunity to take out the commander who controls this city," he said in a pleading tone.

The elf and I finally reached the bottom of the staircase. We were in a meeting room with papers scattered on a table and a chair, which looked to have been thrown. "This is where we were discussing our attack, but now we just need your army to keep the defensive troops distracted—and you, to help us get into the observatory in the uppermost part of the city."

I agreed with a soft nod, and he gave me a slight smile. "Follow me."

He gave another whistle, and a door opened across the room from the staircase.
It was a corridor.
I followed him into the darkness; the torches erupted into light.
"We have a tunnel that leads straight to the center of the city. As far as we know, the Imperials don't know of its existence."

We approached a ladder and a hatch with light beaming through.
"I believe the commander's name is Cassian Vale," the elf said quietly, bitterly.
I began to climb up, pulled up my hood, and readied myself.
Then I followed him up the ladder.

The hatch was in the northern part of the city, not far from the observatory in the center.
We tried to keep a low profile and make it to the observatory, which gleamed in the high moonlight.

Once we got to the entrance, I waved the elves off into the shadows and motioned for the leader to follow behind.
"I'll clear the way. You follow. Watch my back," I whispered.
He nodded and pulled up his mask.

I took a deep breath and closed my eyes while I focused on clearing my mind.
I heard the whistle of the trees, songs of the crickets, the croaking of the frogs—and the screams of my people.
I opened my eyes and headed inside.
He gasped at my sudden disappearance.

I walked about the foyer freely.
There were two guards by the stairs.
I pulled my dagger and walked up behind them.

I grabbed one and slit his throat, then the other before he could gasp.

The elf ran for the stairs, and with a flick of my cloak, I followed.
We headed up four flights of stairs before we entered the main room of the observatory.
It was built with high metal ceilings and large windows in every direction.

It's said that those who control Sylhalin control the eyes of Rhova.

A man in white and golden armor stood humming to himself, looking at the ruins of the city.
I growled and approached him in my ghost-like form.

"Who goes there!?" the commander yelled, pulling his sword and turning toward the stairs.

I stopped dead in my tracks and watched as he walked to the stairs and discovered my elven accomplice.

"Well, well, well. Are you here to kill me? All alone?" the man asked, seeming amused by the events.

The elf began to glare daggers at the man, and the commander just responded with a menacing chuckle, aggressively pulling the elf toward the window by his shirt collar.

"You see that?
That right there is the right way to enforce law.
People don't listen unless some blood is spilled," the commander whispered.

I moved closer to the commander, and with each step, he'd turn to face me and hold the elf defensively.

The commander narrowed his eyes and began to inhale.
"You aren't alone." He smiled and let out a loud chuckle.
"Hello, Verath.
Have you come to admire the view with my new friend and I?" he asked playfully.

I glared.
I didn't know the man, but he knew me—and that was more than enough reason to take him down.

I took a calm breath and emerged from my place in the spirit world.

"Ah, there you are," the man said with a contented sigh.
"Let's just do this. You know you don't stand a chance anyway," he said with a condescending growl and threw the elf to the side, readying his sword.

I lowered my hood, put away my dagger. I was going to let him kick his own ass.

He charged and slashed his sword, destroying a bookshelf in his wake.
I jumped over him, focused my breathing, and raised my hand.

The elf watched from the wall as my vision went green and I became full of rage.
I let out a cry and lowered my hand, and a group of undead soldiers rose to my sides.

"ATTACK!" I shouted, ordering them toward the commander.

The soldiers shimmered light green as the moonlight passed through the observatory's glass ceiling.
They raised their swords and shields and fought the commander.

He put up quite a fight, but in the end, he was outmanned and overpowered.

Finally, one of my soldiers cornered him, grabbed him by the back of his head, and jammed the sword through his throat in an upward thrust.

He gurgled as blood filled his airway and spewed from the neck wound. He fell to his knees.
Then face down on the floor.

The soldiers sheathed their blades and stepped toward me in silent unity. They bowed—and as they vanished into the moonlight, the cold rushed into my bones. It always did, every time I used my abilities, I remembered my master from long ago telling me,
"Remember Verath, abuse of your connection with the spirits will only drive you to madness. If the spirits use you as a conduit too often, you'll lose yourself to them, forever."
To this day I questioned it but always believed it was to scare me.

I raised my hood and walked over to the elf.
I extended a hand, and he took it and stood, in disbelief—as if shocked to be alive.

He looked at me, eyes wide, and asked, "What… are you?"

I sighed.
"I'm just a man with a strong connection to the dead,
I bring those who have lost touch with mortal soil back."

His expression shifted from fear to uncomfortable awe.
"You're a deathwalker…" he asked softly.

He walked over to the window and glanced down at the city, watching as the last of the imperial soldiers fled toward the other kingdoms.

The elven archers took to the rooftops and prevented a few from getting away.

The elf hesitated for a breath, glancing at me with something close to reverence. Then he smiled and ran for the stairs.

As we left the building, the moon sat low on the horizon, and the sun was beginning to rise.
We looked out over the city and watched as the elves claimed victory over the kingdom of Sylhalin.

I looked at the elf.
"We must prepare.
They'll attempt to retaliate and try to reclaim the Spectre," I said with a wry smile.

It wouldn't be long before we had a real leg up on the enemy.

The elf extended a hand. "It was a pleasure fighting with you, Verath," he said with a satisfied smile.

I shook his hand.
"Likewise," I replied.

I narrowed my eyes and realized he hadn't told me his name.

He smiled warmly. "I'm Sam."

As if reading my mind—or my face.

I'm still unsure which.

Act II: Before the Fire Went Out

The city had quieted.

For the first time in a week, no one screamed. No flames licked through rooftops. No blades scraped down alleys. Just wind. Just breathing. Just the hush that settles after too many people survive something they weren't supposed to.

I stayed on the observatory terrace. Below, Sylhalin moved like something wounded. Clerics and laborers picked through the streets with gloved hands, dragging bodies to the pyres. Most of the dead were soldiers. Some weren't. They burned them in timed shifts, to keep smoke low and panic lower.

They said it was to prevent further spread of disease. I said nothing.

Sam sat close—closer than usual. His shoulder nearly brushed mine as he leaned forward, elbows on his knees, carving something from a chunk of scaffold wood. He didn't ask for permission to sit beside me. He just did. And I didn't stop him.

"Are you always this quiet after victory?" he asked.

He didn't look over. "You don't really want the answer to that." I said in a low tone.

“Try me,” he said.

He shrugged. “Feels like we buried something to earn this peace. Something we won’t get back.”

He didn’t reply.

He glanced at me. “Not that you’d lose sleep over it. Don’t pretend you don't have a legend around you, when you walk in a room, most people know what you've done to get there.” Sam’s words stung, but he wasn't wrong.

“Would you? Lose sleep?” I asked defensively.

He nodded. “Yeah. Sometimes. I don't enjoy war; I just want it over with the least amount of casualties.”

I looked back down over the terrace railing. A young cleric was retching behind a wall, her apron soaked. The corpse fires were struggling to keep up. Someone had to clean the mess I’d made.

“It won’t last,” I said, wanting to promise it’d be quick, but didn't want to lie either.

“Doesn’t have to. Just has to mean something.” his tone sunk like a stone after skipping over water.

I scoffed. “Mean what, like hope?”

“No,” he said. “Like effort.”

The carving in his hands was taking shape. Something winged. Rough around the edges. A bird, or maybe a broken thing that used to fly.

“You didn’t have to stay, if you or your people don't want to help, you are free to leave.” I said aggressively.

“I know.” he said softly.

“You could’ve gone east. Found safer work for Queen Cilmair of Lolem.” I stated.

“I could’ve,” he said. “But then who’d be here to stop you from tripping over your own ego?” a smile curled up on his face, as he maintained eye contact with his carving.

I almost smiled. Almost.

He looked at me then—actually looked. And I didn’t look away.

“Have you ever thought about leaving?” I asked.

“Sure,” he said. “Sometimes I even get as far as the door.”

“And?” I asked defensively.

"And I remember you don't know what the hell you're doing, and someone ought to make sure you don't burn the world just because no one taught you how to hold it." He stated firmly.

He set the carving between us. Not offered—just placed. Close enough, I could take it if I wanted to.

"I know I'm not going to change you," he said. "But I think you could still choose to change yourself. And if you ever do—I want to be around to see it." He said with a polite smile.

He stood slowly. No bow. No dramatic exit.

"I'll be downstairs if you need someone to argue with," he stated.

He walked off, leaving me with silence and the shape he'd carved. I didn't touch it. But I wanted to. And behind me, in the decorative fireplace, the last ember of my fire hissed out.

Chapter 8: Let Them Call It Freedom

Act I: Revolution

It had been a week and a half since the siege. The city seemed brighter than it did before—maybe it was the lack of sounds of combat on the wind. I watched from the Sylhalin observatory as the city's white brick streets glimmered beneath the midday sun. Since the remaining imperial troops had been forced out, life had flooded back in—homes and shops restored, elves repainting houses in brilliant, defiant colors. For a fleeting moment, it almost felt like hope.

Yet beneath that hope, a tightness lived in my chest. As I turned away from the window, I couldn't shake the gnawing anxiety. My council believed our victory was secure, but I knew how thin the line was between triumph and catastrophe. If I lost my hold here—if the city slipped from my fingers—everything we'd fought for might collapse. The Empire would seize on any weakness. The world—*my world*—was always a single step from disaster. My council in Ciron told me coming alone was a bad idea, maybe. Just *maybe* they were right.

Footsteps echoed up the winding stairs. I turned to see Sam, now clad in new armor bearing the Eîthorian symbol. The metal caught the light, shining with promise. He looked every bit the proud ally, though he still stood barely to my shoulder. I managed a nod of approval. This was the best choice he could've made. Sylhalin needed to see us as protectors, not conquerors. But I still felt the weight of every decision pressing against my ribs.

Leaving the observatory, I wandered through the city. The elves had returned to the streets—shops flung open, laughter rising. Yet beneath the surface, tension simmered.

As I reached the central fountain, its crystal centerpiece refracting sunlight into shifting colors, a crowd had already gathered.

Their leader stood atop a battered wooden crate. Even caked in dust, he drew every eye—broad-shouldered, bearded, his presence magnetic. There was a hard edge to him, the kind that comes from surviving on nothing but stubbornness and grit. His voice boomed over the murmuring crowd:

"Sylhalin has shed one chain only to be shackled with another! We do not need the Light or the Dark! This is our city—ours to govern, ours to defend!"

The crowd surged, voices rising in support. The protest swept through the city, collecting more supporters with every step. I trailed just ahead of the mob, watching unease bloom on their faces. Had we truly liberated them—or simply traded one ruler for another?

I hurried back to the observatory ignoring the hard weight in my sinking stomach. instructing the guards to hold the doors. Inside, I found Sam arranging chairs at a long table.

"You're early. Council doesn't meet for another half-hour," he said.

I leaned in and quietly told him about the gathering mob. Sam listened, then shrugged. "The city's taken the change well. They just need time."

But as we peered from the south-facing window, the mob stormed the plaza—now armed, voices swelling into a furious tide. Sam's confidence wavered.

Soon after, our council assembled: Sam, Virmath, Laurel, and two unfamiliar men. The mob battered at the doors, the pounding echoing through every stone. My pulse raced—I could not let my fear show; I kept my shaking hands below the table.

The doors burst open, and the mob spilled into the observatory. Soldiers moved to shield us, but I lifted a hand.

"No one dies at our hand unless provoked." I stated firmly.

Their leader—the one from the battered crate—strode forward. Up close, his presence was even more striking: sharp eyes, a jaw clenched with resolve, knuckles scraped raw from hard labor. His name was Eldric, and he spoke for them all.

"You claim you freed us," Eldric said, "but all you've done is replace one yoke with another. Your soldiers still walk our streets. Your curfews still hold us back. We want liberation, not occupation."

My insides twisted. I wanted to believe our cause was righteous, but I saw the fear and exhaustion behind his defiance.

"Without my garrison, Sylhalin is exposed. The Empire could return. We keep order—for your safety." I said, trying to persuade the mob.

Eldric stepped closer, voice steady but fierce.

"You cannot trade one oppressor for another. End martial law. Let the elves of Sylhalin govern themselves. If you want trust, you must give it."

Laurel spoke up, her tone gentle but firm.

"They have a point. We can't win them as allies if we rule by force."

I stared at Eldric. He reminded me of the mountain itself—unyielding, immovable.

"If I withdraw my soldiers, you guarantee order. No riots. No chaos. You keep Sylhalin free—even if the Light Empire comes knocking."

He met my gaze, unblinking.

"You have my word. Sylhalin will stand ready. But not as your puppet. As your *equal.*"

The council was silent. My hands trembled at my sides, invisible beneath the table. If I lost Sylhalin, the campaign could fail. But if I crushed these people—I'd already lost.

"Very well," I said at last, forcing my fear behind a mask of command. "Martial law ends today. Sylhalin governs itself alongside my council, but know this—if you betray that trust, if chaos returns, I will act."

A beat passed. Then relief, disbelief, and celebration erupted in the chamber. Eldric gripped my hand—strong and unyielding.

"We'll remember this, King of Ciron."

As the crowd filed out, Sam let out a breath he'd been holding.

"You did the right thing," he murmured.

I gave a noncommittal grunt, anxiety still churning inside me.

Back at the council table, Laurel raised a new topic.

"If we can rally the villages in the Sarnawenian Forest, we might finally bring down both the Queen of Sarnawen and Rostov of Zodan."

Virmath rolled his eyes, but even he managed a grudging nod. The meeting ended as gracefully as possible under the circumstances.

As I retreated to my quarters, Sam caught up to me.

"Verath! Care for a celebratory brew?"

I managed a wry smile.

"You should work out more. No knight should be winded by four flights of stairs." I said playfully.

He scowled, then grinned.

"Let's go celebrate!"
As we left the observatory, the city buzzed with new freedom. But I could not shake the sense of foreboding—

the feeling that the peace we'd bought was fragile as glass. One misstep, and the world would burn again.

Act II: Before We Begin to Break

We sat on the steps outside the council hall. The marble still held heat from the day, but the city had cooled. A breeze rolled through the lower courts, scattering petals from a newly replanted garden. The sky had just begun to violet.

Sam handed me a drink. Nothing strong. Just something warm. Probably stolen from Laurel's storage—she'd notice, and she'd forgive him. She always did.

"I've never seen you hesitate before," he said, not looking at me.

I didn't answer.

"Today," he continued. "In the observatory. You looked like you were going to say no."

"I was." I said.

He nodded like that made sense.

"Why didn't you?" he asked.

"Because there's no one left to fight that won't cost me the city." I explained.

"That's not the same as doing the right thing."

“No,” I said quietly. “It isn’t.”

He rested his forearms on his knees, the cup turning slow in his hands.

The silence between us was strange. Not uncomfortable. Just… weighted. Like we were both hearing something neither of us wanted to name.

“Do you think it’s working?” I asked. “What we’re doing?”

“I think,” he said carefully, “you’re trying. And I think trying means more than people want to admit.”

“I could’ve killed Eldric.” I said firmly.

“You could’ve killed a lot of people.” He said quietly.

I gave a small breath of something that might’ve been a laugh.

“I still might.”

He bumped his shoulder gently against mine.

“Then I’ll be here to stop you.”

He waited a beat, then added:

“Careful. Wouldn’t want you to trip over that ego of yours,” Sam said with a wink.

I scoffed.

“Didn’t you use that line already?”

“Yeah,” he said. “But it keeps being true.” he rolled his eyes playfully.

We sat like that for a while. The city quiet. The streetlamps flickering to life. Somewhere, someone sang too loud off-key. It didn’t matter.

“I should go over the plans, I need to think of a way to begin my search for the heiress.” I said eventually.

“You should rest.” He said softly.

I looked at him. He was still watching the garden, the petals drifting like ash. His expression unreadable. Gentle. Sad, maybe.

“You’re not going to stay long, are you?” I asked.

He turned then. Met my eyes.

“I’ll stay long enough.”

That was the closest either of us got to saying it.

Maybe he was my moral compass, out of everyone under my command, Sam seemed to be one of the few to tell me like it is, I hadn't realized how much I respected that approach.

Part II: We Were Not Whole, But We Were Here

Chapter 9: Home

I walked through the forest near Rostov's camp. The cub followed not far behind, lifting his paws in a goofy little walk. I let out a giggle and continued toward my snares—the last few had come up empty, but I was hoping for at least a rabbit or two. The cub might be smaller than most, but he was always famished.

I entered a small clearing and saw I'd caught a fairly large rabbit and a small squirrel. I started untying the cottontail as the cub marched to the squirrel and began to eat. I giggled and patted him on the head.

"I'm going to have to give you a name, little one." I said quietly.

He growled as he ripped apart the squirrel. I reset the snare, placed the rabbit in my pack, pulled out a piece of cloth, wrapped the leftover squirrel meat, and tucked it away. I clicked my tongue and headed toward the house, the cub following close behind.

After just about a week and a half, he already seemed to be getting bigger—maybe it was all the food. Or maybe it was some sense of safety. I'd been giving him entire animals, trying to ensure he was fed with prey as close to living as I could manage, without putting him in danger.

I walked up the path to the house and opened the door. Drake sat at the table, reading an old book he had found our first night here. I went to the makeshift fire pit we'd built in the fireplace, set up the rack, and lit a flame. It began to grow. I pulled out the rabbit and headed to the kitchen counter, starting to clean it. After a few minutes, I had fresh meat ready for the fire.

Drake looked up from his book and inhaled deeply.

"That smells delicious," he said as I placed the meat on the rack. "I just started it; how can you smell it already?" I said with a chuckle, like the cub, he too was always famished.

The cub mewled softly and curled into my lap as I sat by the fire. I petted him, listening to the crackling flame.

I looked to Drake as I packed up the cooked meat.

"What about Atlas?" I asked curiously.

Drake looked up from his book, confused. "I'm sorry?" he said.

I turned my gaze to the tiger cub sleeping near the fire. Drake smiled and nodded.

"One that suffers or endures," he said, turning back to his book.

I sat down beside the cub.

"*Atlas*. It fits *you,*" I whispered.

Atlas stretched, yawned, and drifted back into sleep. I smiled and petted him as he rested. As I looked down at the tiny life in my lap, I thought about how he must feel—safe, loved, protected. Home.

Home. The word carried so much weight. It wasn't the castle, or the village, or the woods. It was moments like this: sharing warmth, a meal, or laughter with someone who cared—or even someone you were just beginning to trust. The cub and Drake… they were growing on me, each in their own way, it had only been a week and a half. It surprised me how much I wanted to keep them both safe.

I woke Atlas and stood up. I grabbed my gear and picked him up.

"Where are you going?" Drake asked.

I turned and said, "Home."

Drake grabbed his pack and staff. I'd made him his staff out of an old candlestick, snapping off the feet so he had a blunt metal weapon. Drake refused a sword. He once told me, "I'm more of a pacifist." But when it mattered, I knew he may kill.

He picked up the knife I'd used off the counter.

"Ew, you left rabbit goo on my blade," he said, wiping it on his pants.

We headed outside, making our way toward the Castle of Zodan—Rostov's old stronghold. He'd abandoned it not long after taking up hunting. A small village seemed to have formed around the castle.

Atlas wiggled in my arms, so I set him down. He walked ahead of me. As we moved, the forest began to thin, and we reached a steep hill. The castle sat in the clearing below. Small houses dotted the area around it; people wandered through the settlement, tending to daily life. They didn't look like military—hopefully we could pass through without trouble.

I picked up Atlas and slid down the hillside cautiously. At the bottom, I set him down. He mewled softly.

Drake and I walked through the outskirts of the village, watching people talk, laugh, and live in simple huts beneath a towering castle on a high cliff above. It was a strange contrast—peace beside ruin.

We moved past the village and continued toward Khofte, following the edge of the cliffs near Eîthor. The valley below had plenty of fires speckled through it, I couldn't help but wonder why. The path we followed wound up into the mountainous kingdom. Dragons soared overhead, their priests guiding them in the art of flight.

We passed through three villages. At last, I stopped at the cliffside and watched the ocean. Drake came up behind me and sat beside me. He looked between the castle behind us sitting on the opposite cliff behind me and the village.

"Is this your home?" Drake asked softly. "I thought you said it didn't exist anymore."

I sighed. "Technically, it doesn't."

I shook my head and reached into my pack, pulling the squirrel meat. I set it beside Atlas. He ate happily.

I pointed toward the ocean. As the sun set, it glinted against the water—just enough to reveal what lay beneath: the windows, the stained glass of the church, the rooftops of my home. Dark, wavy shapes beneath the waves. Drake's eyes widened, but he said nothing.

We just sat there and watched the sunset.

The next thing I remembered, Atlas was curled up on my chest. I blinked awake, then sat up on the edge of the cot, wiping my eyes and running my fingers through my hair to untangle it. Drake snored on the cot nearby.

I stood, grabbed a chunk of bread from a nearby plate, and threw it at his face.

"I'M UP!" he shouted, as he rolled off the cot onto the floor.

I smirked, grabbed my pack and sword, and noticed Count Dendrin had left a few slices of meat for Atlas. I left the plate by the cub, and he began to devour it.

I wrapped my scarf around my neck and covered my mouth and nose. Drake groaned as he sat up, his hair wild, a slab of meat still stuck to his cheek.

I approached Dendrin outside the guest house.

"Thank you for your generosity these past few days. We appreciate it," I said.

Dendrin gleamed. "You're very welcome, Akira. I'm always happy to help—it is God's will," he said with a bow.

I bowed in return.

"You should come back more often. I know it's hard for you because of what happened to your mother, but those of us who remain mourn your absence. You could even stay in the castle with my family and me. We care for you; you are family after all." he added.

Drake wandered outside and joined us, the meat still stuck to his face, half-asleep but fully geared up. I giggled and smiled at him but turned back to Dendrin.

"No, thank you. Your guest house is more than enough—and you've been more than generous to me since the raid," I said, bowing again.

Dendrin turned and headed toward the center of the village.

"I have to get to Afternoon Mass, but it was good to see you," he said, wrapping me in a hug before disappearing down the path to the church.

Not long after, the clock tower rang out—twelve chimes. Noon.

Drake peeled the meat off his face, one eye still closed. Atlas leapt up and devoured it in one gulp.

"*Ew*... Who was that guy?" he asked sleepily.

I smiled and patted Atlas.

"That's Count Dendrin. He's the lord of Khofte. After the raid on my village, the other children and I were taken by Imperials—trained as child soldiers. Only a few of us survived."

I took a breath.

"Dendrin led the search for us. He freed us, settled down, and became a cleric. He took care of me for a while, until I was ready to go out on my own. He's my family now." I said softly.

As we made our way back down the mountain of Zodan, climbing the hills. We passed near Rostov's old camp but just as I had thought we had managed to avoid attention.

"HALT!"

A voice rang out from behind. Drake and I turned, his staff already raised. A man in a deep blue cloak over chainmail approached, sword drawn. He was flanked by paladins, clerics, knights, and mystics—eight in total. The man had a light beard, a scar beneath his right eye, and a deep, commanding voice.
"Drop your weapons. I won't say it again." He ordered.
Drake raised his staff higher. I pulled out my katana.

"No," I said firmly, hoping my tone would be as commanding as my heartbeat.

Chapter 10: The Cursed Heart of Magic

"Drop your weapons. I won't say it again!" I ordered, my voice echoing off the trees.

The man on the right, in tattered clothes, raised his staff, ready to strike. The woman, scarf covering her face, drew her sword and glanced at him. He didn't move, but she answered calmly, her tone steely and unwavering.

"*No.*"

My eyes made contact with hers, her gaze showing as much might as her stance, something in me tingled, I wasn't sure what it was, but there's something about her. I snapped my fingers, and my knights advanced. Each took on a member of the pair. The woman killed her attacker with a single, clean swing—decapitating him. The man moved with startling speed, taking two swift strikes to knock his knight unconscious. The rest of my group tensed.

I raised my hand to call them off. No sense in sacrificing more comrades to two strangers who clearly knew how to handle themselves. Besides, no ordinary knight can enter Ectwë anyway.

"I don't see a reason to lose more good men today," I said firmly.

I took a steadying breath and focused my magic. From the fallen knight's corpse, a spirit rose—hollow-eyed and silent— glowing in a solid dark green hue and stood before me. It bowed, then joined our ranks, awaiting my command.

"Subdue them. No further bloodshed," I instructed the spirit.

The spirit nodded, binding the woman's wrists in glowing cuffs. Her companion tried to intervene, but his hand passed through the spirit. Both soon stood disarmed and restrained, glaring daggers at me.

"See? That wasn't so hard," I said, trying to keep my tone even.

Their eyes told me exactly what they thought of that.

I turned toward the winding path that led to Lord Rostov's encampment. My followers fell in behind me.

We reached the camp—a cluster of long, stone cells lined the path, beyond which sat an assortment of tents, large and small. The restrained man in my company seemed uneasy as we entered Rostov's camp.

A man sprinted out from behind a tent, a crossbow leveled at my head. Before he could fire, one of my paladins, Sara, raised her shield. He slammed into it face-first and collapsed. She stepped forward, seized him by the neck, and demanded.

“WHERE IS ROSTOV?” she asked firmly.

The man sputtered, panic in his eyes.
“I—I won’t t-tell… y-you… nothing…!”

She ripped a ring of keys from his belt and dragged him along the row of cages until she stopped at one containing a restless jaguar. She turned the key in the lock and glanced at the man, whose eyes widened in terror.

“NOOOOO—PLEASE!” he whimpered.

She slammed him against the bars. After a tense moment, she let him drop, watching him crumple to his knees, sobbing.

“I honestly think he doesn’t know,” she said, disgusted, tossing the keys aside.

I sighed, pinching the bridge of my nose. Why can’t anything ever be straightforward?

Behind me, the two prisoners whispered urgently. I whirled and seized the man by his collar. The woman immediately stepped in, eyes blazing.

“Drop him. Now.” She ordered.

"You're not in a position to make demands," I said, voice low. I met the man's eyes. "What did you just say to her?"

He looked at the woman. She gave a tiny nod.

"Rostov and his men were heading for Sylhalin as of yesterday morning," he said quickly. "That guy you just floored wouldn't know much. He was knocked out before we got here."

I released him and turned to Sam, now my trusted lieutenant.

"Do you think our guards can hold off Rostov's men?" I asked under my breath.

Sam grimaced. "Maybe his men—but not Rostov himself. He's… dangerous."

I exhaled, rubbing my eyes. "I knew it was a bad idea to trust the elves to self-govern." I said with a deep sigh.

"So, you're sure they were headed for Sylhalin?" I asked the prisoners.

They both nodded.
"There was some kind of explosion inside the walls, there's been a lot of activity over that kingdom the past few days." the man added. "Balls of flame rained over the

city just a week ago?" he looked to the woman accompanying him for confirmation, she gave a nod.

My mind raced, anxiety tightening my chest. If we lost Sylhalin now, everything we'd built could collapse.

"We move on," I said, forcing my voice to stay level. "Ectwë isn't far. Let's see if we can find anything about the heiress."

Sam relayed the order. The group stirred.

I turned to the prisoners just as a strange sound rustled from the woman's pack.

"What's that?" I demanded, grabbing her bag before she could react. She tensed, poised to strike.

Inside, I found a tiger cub—its eyes wide, fur bristling with fear. My breath caught. Tiger cubs were nearly extinct.

She glared at me, fierce protectiveness blazing in her gaze. I gently set the pack on the ground in front of her, careful not to startle the cub further.

The hair on my neck stood on end. The woman could become a problem if she senses they're in danger. Nothing more dangerous than a cornered matriarch.

"Release their chains," I said quietly.

Sam leaned in. "Are you sure? They did kill Duran."

I nodded. "We need all the help we can get."

Sam complied, unlocking their cuffs.

"You don't get your weapons back just yet," I warned. "Help us, and you'll be free to go."

The woman exchanged a look with her companion, then nodded once.
"With weapons, we're better assets," she said—calm but edged with defiance.

I paused, then signaled the paladin to return their blades and staff. I don't know what it was, but I acquiesced to the request.

She knelt and offered a piece of dried meat to the cub—Atlas, I guessed, from her soft whispers.

The man stepped forward, extending his hand—almost cheerful.
"I'm Drake. This is Akira, and the cub is Atlas."

Sam introduced our own group.
"This is King Verath." he beamed with matching energy.

Drake beamed and extended a hand.
"Pleasure to meet you."

I nodded, trying to muster a polite smile, but my mind was already spinning through contingencies.

Sam whispered an apology for my abruptness.
"He's a good man. Just… focused." Drake nodded, "I understand, she's the same way." he said softly nodding his head towards Akira, she responded with a firm elbow to his side. He laughed softly as she did it.

We pushed on toward the cursed forest of Ectwë.

As we reached a derelict house at the forest's edge, I addressed the company.

"No one without strong magical resistance can enter. Akira, Drake, Sam—you'll need to stay close to the paladins. Their wards will protect you. The rest of you, stay alert. The trees here attack when threatened. We're searching for any trace of the heiress. Move carefully."

I also dispatched a strike team—two mystics and a ranger—to flank ahead and scout from the north ridge. If there were orcs, I wanted them cornered.

They nodded. We entered the woods.

Sunlight faded fast, and the trees shimmered with eerie hues—blue, red, pink, green—their bark twisted into faces reflecting every imaginable emotion. The path narrowed, undergrowth thickened. Vivid green puddles bubbled beside us.

The trees watched. Drake seemed uneasy. I watched him closely.

A man came screaming from the shadows. Roots burst from the ground, seizing him. He struggled, but the hand of roots dragged him down. His screams cut off in an instant.

The group shuddered, casting uneasy glances at me.

“Keep moving,” I snapped, masking my unease.

We slid down a low hill and pressed on, the trail vanishing beneath us until we stumbled into a clearing of ruined buildings and charred corpses.

Low voices drifted from the shadows. I raised my hand in silence.

Two men stood with their backs turned, one gnawing on an arm like it was a turkey leg. I motioned the group to cover and slipped to the next ruin.

Sam hissed from behind Sara, “What are those things?!” he said in a worried whisper.

Drake’s voice was tight. “Orcs. Witches created them in the First Age; they protected the village before *‘The Last Resort.’*” I looked at Drake, watching his face suspiciously, Akira elbowed him, and they had a hushed conversation before I could infer what that meant.

I scanned the next clearing—more orcs, drinking and laughing, oblivious to us. No way we’d pass unnoticed.

“We’ll have to clear them,” I muttered.

Akira crept to the edge of the paladin’s magical ward attempting to join me, jaw set.
“How many are there?” she whispered.

“Nine—eleven, counting the two behind us.” I stated.

She tried to hand her pack to Drake.

“What are you doing?” he whispered, alarmed.

“I can take them out,” she said, checking her blade.

“You’ll get yourself killed, you need the ward's protection, I’ll go.” he hissed, panic in his eyes.

“No. She stated you’re no safer without the ward either.” She said menacingly.

She was wild-eyed now, frantic—like she’d seen this before. Like losing him again wasn’t an option.

They whispered in fierce tension.

I motioned to Duran’s spirit, a paladin, and two mystics. “Circle around. Handle the rest.”

They nodded and vanished into the gloom.

I drew my dagger, shifting into a spectral haze, Drake gasped at my disappearance. “Yeah, he does that.” Sam said reassuringly. I crept up behind the nearest orc. One swift plunge to the head—and chaos erupted.

The orcs grabbed weapons, roaring in confusion. Fire exploded from the undergrowth. Vines lashed out, dragging orcs into the earth for disturbing the land's peace. Duran’s spirit impaled one, then another. Within minutes, we’d cleared the village.

I sent the group to search the ruins for signs of the heiress and moved to check on the others.

As I neared the first ruined building, I heard shouting. I crept forward and saw two orcs bearing down on Sara, who shielded herself, Akira, and Sam behind a glowing barrier.

Drake lay outside it—motionless.

Sam looked shaken, still clutching his sword.
"He came out of nowhere—I panicked," he said, eyes wide, as I approached, he spoke to me, like I could protect him.

Akira glared at him.
"Like an idiot." She said,

I dispatched the orcs with haste and knelt by Drake, heart tight in my chest.

I reached and gripped his wrist. It was cool, but there was a pulse. Weak—but alive.

Akira dropped to her knees beside him, attempting to grab his hand like it was the last rope tethering her to sanity. As her hand exited the barrier her hand glowed a shade of green turning black, she yelped in pain, she and Sam pulled her hand back to safety. "I told you, no ordinary person could enter without the ward, Ectwë doesn't care about your grief.

Relief swept over me, Drake was alive. But tension still thickened the air.

Chapter 11: Some Things You Only Learn Once

Act I: The Blood Wasn't Just Mine

I felt so helpless, being trapped in a bubble while Drake was unconscious and in harm's way. The more worked up I got, the more Atlas began to get nervous, squirming around in my pack. Sam turned to me and tried to explain himself, but I didn't want to hear it—I tuned him out and asked Verath about Drake.

He turned and said, "There's a pulse. He's alive."

I took a breath and tried not to kill Sam where he stood. Verath tasked the paladin with keeping Drake safe until he woke.

"I want to help," I said. "I am better off helping than being trapped in here."

Verath shook his head. "Not happening," he replied. "Wasn't feeling the acidic touch of the spirits enough for you? Stay put."

I growled under my breath and watched as one of the Mystics called for Verath. He walked off, and I was left with those of us in the barrier. I slid my back down the wall, sat, and waited for Drake to wake. Sam tried to sit next to me, but I pulled my katana and held the tip to his throat.

He gulped and stepped back.

Drake groaned and grasped his head. "Wha…t… happen…ed?" he asked between breaths.

I crawled over to him, lowered my scarf, and smiled lightly. "You're okay," I said.

The paladin stared at her hand and scoffed as I said it. I turned my gaze to her. "You have something to say?" I asked her.

She rolled her eyes and went back to her hand. I stood up and approached the paladin. She looked at me with an irritated scowl.

"What?!" I snapped.

I pulled my katana and held it to her neck. The paladin smiled and stepped into my blade.

"DO IT! YOU CAN'T GET OUT OF HERE WITHOUT ME!" she screamed tauntingly.

I pulled back my sword, but as I did, Sam jumped in front and shouted, "*NO!*" I turned to retaliate but before I knew it.

My sword ripped through him, separating him in two. We all gasped. Sam landed at two sides of the barrier. We all stood in silence as he let out one last breath. Drake sat up and looked at me as if I knew what to do next.

Blood. So much blood. It seeped into the magical soil beneath my boots only solidifying my shock. What have I done? I didn't mean to.

The paladin shoved me away, grabbed my pack and ran, taking the barrier with her. "*Hey!" She took Atlas!*

I pulled up my scarf and covered my face and fought to pursue her, but the air was still heavy. I struggled to pull in each breath, and quickly tried to follow her, but collapsed to my knees, and watched the paladin run up the hill and eventually out of sight. After that, I only remember flashes—being carried past the colorful trees, my view shifting in every direction. I was being carried; I tried to fight it, but I couldn't even breathe, let alone fight. My vision went black.

"*HEY!*" Drake yelled. "*He's not yours!"*

I woke up to my body hitting the ground. I fought to get my eyes open. I watched Drake tackle the paladin just outside the forest, grabbing his staff and whacking her on the head. She fell back to the ground, unconscious. I tried to get up but failed, watching Drake Walk over and drag me toward the unconscious paladin.

I could hear the waterfall just up ahead. Drake leaned me up against a rock and then walked over to prop the paladin up against another rock across from me, Drake came over and set my pack next to me, Atlas popped his head out curiously. Drake crouched in front of me, struggling to keep a smile.

"How are you feeling?" he asked.

I nodded my head lightly, the fog seemed to have lasting effects, no wonder people avoided the center of the forest.

"Great," he replied softly.

"YOU IDIOTS! YOU KILLED VERATH'S RIGHT-HAND MAN, WE'RE ALL DEAD! HAVEN'T YOU HEARD THE STORIES!? HE'S CRAZY! WE'RE SO DEAD!" the paladin shrieked, her voice cracked and shrill.

Drake froze. His eyes flicked toward me, then back to the paladin. His grip tightened on the staff in his hand.

He took a step closer. "You need to calm down," he said, voice shaking slightly.

She didn't. "HE'S GOING TO SLAUGHTER US! I WAS HIS ELITE! DO YOU KNOW WHAT YOU'VE DONE? WHAT I'VE DONE?!" Her voice broke into hysterical sobs, screaming up at the sky. "He trusted me!" In her hysteria she leaped from her spot across from me and was right in my face screaming, she gripped my head and slammed it into the rock behind me. I was caught off guard and too weak to fight back. My hands found her face and I pushed with all my remaining strength.

Drake clenched his jaw. "Stop!"

But she wouldn't. "IT WASN'T SUPPOSED TO BE LIKE THIS! I DIDN'T SIGN UP FOR—"

WHAM. my head hit the rock again.

He struck her, once to match the blow.

WHAM. I began to see stars, in a daze.

Again. He matched her efficiency.

WHAM. The wind flooded from my lungs as I was thrown into the rock once more.

And again, until her cries stopped, her body slack and still.

The staff dropped from his hands as he collapsed to his knees in front of her broken form. Blood pooled beneath her collapsed skull. The silence roared.

I struggled to get to him and eventually knelt beside him. I was dizzy and weak but knew he needed me.

I placed my hand on his back.

He flinched. "She was one of his people," he whispered. "I didn't want to—she just—"

He cut himself off, pulling away, hating himself already. I could feel the rage emanating from his body, as he ran off towards the top of the waterfall.

I stood up, wobbly, but otherwise fine, my head was bleeding, I ripped up some cloth I had in my pack and wrapped it around my head. and approached the beaten corpse leaning against the rock. I shuddered at her collapsed skull. There was yelling coming from the cursed forest of Ectwë. I grabbed my gear and ran off after Drake.

Atlas was growling in my pack; I stopped to check on him and found him gnawing on Drake's leather-bound book. I pulled out the book and flipped to the first page. I read the first page and realized it was a diary, someone's entry.

'The village elders are setting a curfew; now at sundown all citizens of Ectwë are to be in their homes with the lights off. They believe that King Rotík is targeting the village. There have been rumors that he has an heiress with a woman in the village. I'm currently writing by candlelight, and Mixa is playing with her bear. I hope that the elders are wrong. The village's last resort is not a pretty one, for anyone.'

The book was filled, each page covered top to bottom. I flipped to the last page.

'The elders are limiting how much magic we can use. It's getting to be less and less each day. Rotík's forces have surrounded the village; most have tried to take us women. One caught me out by the waterfall; I was able to redirect and whip the water at him and get away. Maybe the last resort isn't so bad after all.'

I can't help but wonder what the last resort was, Drake had mentioned it but never elaborated. I put the diary away and fed Atlas the last of the meat I had; I guess I'll need to catch some more rabbits after I find Drake.

I let Atlas Walk with me as we approached the waterfall just west of Zodan. The sound of the water crashing down the four-story drop filled the air as it smashed into the sharp rocks in the lake below. Atlas and I approached the upper-cliffside. There was something up ahead, and as we got closer, I saw it was a man standing at the edge. I ran ahead while Atlas followed not far behind the heavy thud of his paws followed by my frantic steps. The closer I got, the more I came to see it was Drake. I threw down my gear and called to him.

He turned and stepped away.

"Get back!"

I reached my hand out. "Please, don't do this," I said urgently.

He looked at me, tears in his eyes.

"I have to! I don't want to hurt you too!" He started to sob uncontrollably.

I carefully grabbed his hands and held them in mine. "You could never hurt me." I smiled lightly. "In fact, you saved me." I said, trying to help convince him. He pulled down my scarf and traced the cut on my left cheek. I wiped the tears from his face.

"I have a bloodlust," he said in a stifled sob.

I smiled and shrugged. "Well, a little," I said lightly.

He began to chuckle. He gave me a giant smile; he was about to speak when the cliffside crumbled and he plummeted down into the mist below.

"NO!!!" I screamed.

I fell to my knees and searched the fog for signs that he had lived. My hair flowed with the wind, my heart fell to the pit of my stomach, and I knew well by now. He was gone again.

Atlas began nudging my side, but I couldn't move at first. The world was a dull roar in my ears, the cliff's edge cold beneath my palms. I pressed my forehead to the ground, choking on the air, on the taste of loss. My hands curled into the dirt, nails scraping rock.

For a long moment I let the ache in my chest hollow me out. I felt my breathing stutter, tears hot and unwanted burning tracks down my face, and for the first time in years, I wanted to scream. Not from pain, or anger—but from helplessness.

Atlas whimpered, pawing at me, and I pulled him in close, burying my face in his fur. My body shook, the grief swallowing me in waves, as memories—what little I'd shared with Drake, the cautious trust, the warmth around the fire—rushed up to fill the empty space he left behind.

I hated that I'd let him get close, hated that I couldn't stop him from vanishing from my life. The guilt was suffocating, heavy as the night pressing down on me. If

I'd been faster, smarter, if I'd just tried harder, maybe he'd still be here. Maybe I wouldn't be so alone.

Finally, when the tears ran dry and only exhaustion was left, I wiped my face and forced myself to stand. My legs trembled. Atlas kept close, tail low, his wide eyes watching me like I might fall apart at any second. I lifted my hand to his head and gave him a little rub, my voice a ragged whisper.

"Let's go, buddy. We'll check below." I said with a sniffle.

I grabbed my gear and headed down the hill, the moon rising above the Castle of Zodan, to the east. For a fleeting moment, I wondered how Dendrin and his family were. Atlas and I eventually reached the boulder near Ectwë where the corpse had been, but now there was just a blood trail leading into the forest. I didn't even want to know what monstrous thing had taken it. We turned and continued downhill toward the lake at the bottom of the waterfall, but there was no trace of Drake—no blood, no trail, nothing.

I searched for a while, stumbling through the underbrush in the dark, calling his name even though I knew he couldn't answer. Each time the wind rustled, my heart twisted with hope, but it was just the night closing in, swallowing the last of the warmth.

Finally, with Atlas shivering beside me and my limbs heavy with fatigue, I gave up. I sat for a while at the water's edge, watching the black surface for any sign—any ripple, any movement—but the lake was still and silent.

I don't know how long I sat there, only that the night pressed in colder and lonelier than ever. I wrapped Atlas in my cloak and held him tight, refusing to let go of the last living thing I had. And when I finally stood, there was nothing left but the hollow echo of Drake's absence—and the sharp, silent promise that I would find him again. I turned towards the lone path leading straight to Sylhalin, maybe just *maybe*— Drake would follow the path? Before I knew it, Atlas and I began following the barren path to Sylhalin.

Act II: After the Silence

The wind had gone quiet by the time I opened my eyes.

For a moment, I thought I was still dead. The sky was smeared gray above me, and the waterfall's roar felt distant—like the world had shrunk away, muffled by fog. My ribs ached. My head throbbed. I rolled onto my side, coughing, then dragged myself to my feet, water dripped into the soil below me.

"*Akira?*" I croaked. "*Atlas?*"

Nothing.

I staggered forward, slipping on wet grass and broken stone. The earth had crumbled beneath me—how far had I fallen? I couldn't have landed far from the lake, but when I looked around, "breathe, Drake, you're okay." I said quietly to myself, trying to relieve my anxiety, but there was no one. No pack. No cub. No Akira brushing hair from her face or trying to stop me from doing something reckless.

Just silence. I tried to orient myself. I must've been carried away from the lake by the current, I awoke on a riverbed a few meters from the waterfall.

I climbed the hill, legs trembling, heart pounding in my ears. When I crested the ridge where we'd last spoken, the space was empty. Her footprints were faint, already fading. The gear she'd dropped was gone. So was she.

She *left.*

Because of *me…?*

I collapsed to my knees, fingers digging into the damp earth. My hands still felt dirty—bloodied, cursed. I saw the paladin's body every time I blinked. Her skull caved in. My staff slick with red.

I *killed* her.

Not in defense. Not in battle.

Out of *rage.*

Because she hurt *Akira.* Because she wouldn't stop. Because something in me… *snapped.*

I stared at my hands, wondering what they'd become.

She'd said I saved her. But what if I hadn't? What if I'd only shown her the part of me, I'd been trying to bury—the part I didn't want to exist?

Akira had gone. She had every right to. Maybe she was safer that way.

I stood, dragging my staff behind me, and made my way back down the waterfall trail. My legs carried me without thought, only grief. I passed the blood-darkened rocks where we'd landed after escaping the forest, The paladin's corpse was gone. I approached the spot where she held me silently, knowing words would sate me. The place where I ruined everything.

I reached the water's edge.

Nobody.

No sign of her or Atlas.

Nothing to hold onto but guilt.

The forest moaned somewhere behind me. The silence ahead stretched like a warning.

But I couldn't stay.

Not here.

Not in the crater of everything I broke.

The only path that remained? To Sylhalin, if she went, I'd go too. Not because I deserved to see her again—but because I had to believe there was still something left to fix.

I gripped the staff tighter.

And followed the same path I hoped she took.

One step behind.

Always.

Chapter 12: The Rise of New Zodan

"Verath!" Someone shouted.

I turned and found Megan, one of the mystics, holding a leather-bound book. It was heavy with detailed maps and notes about Rotík's search for his heiress. The trail zigzagged across the continent, finally vanishing into the northern ice caps.

Megan met my eyes. "That would've been the safest place for her then," she explained, voice barely above a whisper.

Suddenly, a scream shattered the uneasy peace of the ruined village. "*NO!!*" I spun toward the sound, catching a flash of one of the paladins—*Sara*—running past an alleyway. I apologized to Megan, my feet already moving, and sprinted to investigate.

What I found twisted my gut. Sam, my right hand, lay cut in half on the ground. My spine tingled. "*SAM!*" I dropped to my knees at what was left of him, the pool of blood spreading under my hands. Megan and the others gathered, murmuring in shock and horror.

I closed my eyes, grasping for composure, and focused. With a rush of wind, Sam's translucent spirit appeared before me in a hollow green aura. He looked mournful, then managed a thin smile, nodding up toward the hill before the wind pulled him away.

I didn't follow immediately. I reached into my pocket and withdrew the small carving Sam had made from scaffold wood our first night of camp after leaving Sylhalin—a little dog with crooked ears. I turned it over in my fingers, tracing the shape he'd chiseled smooth. I remembered how proud he'd looked when he'd finished it, how he'd handed it to me without a word and simply sat beside me.

Now he was *dead. Slaughtered.*

My fingers clenched around the carving until my knuckles ached. *Akira*. I could see her face in my mind, calm, composed, playing the part of the weary warrior—but she had murdered him. Not in battle. Not in fear. She killed him like it was nothing. My breath turned sharp in my chest.

She was no survivor. No hero. She was the danger we hadn't seen coming. And she would answer for it.

I rose. "We go that way," I ordered, pointing the group toward the hill. As we neared the forest's edge, the air filled with distant shouting—tension sharp and unspoken.

We crept to the southwest exit of Ectwë. Ahead, I caught sight of Akira, standing by a rock, snatching up her gear before running up the hill toward the waterfall. Her cub trailed close behind.

Our group—Megan, two mystics, a single paladin, and myself—moved into the clearing. The mystics recoiled at the scene: Sara's body, bludgeoned and lying in the dirt, blood pooled in the grass. Megan covered her face and sobbed. "Who would do something like this? No one deserves to be mutilated like this…" her voice shattered like glass.

I reached down, unfastened the golden ring from Sara's finger, and handed it to the other paladin among us, Darion. Megan fell to her knees, pulling at the corpse's arms. "We can't leave her here! Sara deserves better than to rot!" she wailed.

A strange chill crept up my spine. In a blink, Sara's ghost shimmered in a green hue before us, kneeling beside Megan and whispering something that seemed to calm her. Sara's spirit rose, turned toward the trees, and vanished into the wind. "It is my duty to protect the fallen. I must return," she whispered—another soul claimed by the forest.

Megan and the others dragged Sara's body into the trees, their grief palpable in every movement. I started to follow, but something in me pulled toward the lake. Alone with Darion, I descended into the fog beneath the waterfall.

Silence, broken only by the rush of water. I listened—only the whispers of the fallen. For a moment, I wondered if my instincts were failing me, but then a distant explosion flared in the southeast. Colors rained down—a celebration from Khofte, perhaps.

I let myself breathe for a moment, even as my nerves refused to settle. I returned to the camp, where—for a fleeting stretch—there was peace. Megan and her two mystics lingered, the mystics quietly showing off their skills. One drew water from a bucket into a shimmering orb, letting it burst in a soft rain. The other coaxed a small stone figure from the earth, making it twirl like a tiny dancer. The moment felt almost magical—brief shelter from the blood and loss.

But as the fire burned low, Megan approached. "Verath, I think we should detour to Sarnawen," she said softly, clutching the map to her chest. I nodded, feeling numb. "You, and the mystics, go. Stay away from the walls, don't tempt the guards," I told her. She offered a small smile and slipped away, leaving only Darion and myself behind.

The camp felt emptier with each loss. My mind churned with intrusive thoughts. Akira's face flickered in my memory, sharp and unreadable. She killed him. She killed Sam. A dark part of me screamed—*Kill her now. End this before she brings more ruin.*

I clenched my jaw, fighting the urge. If I lost control, if I lashed out, everything I'd built could unravel. The world could fall apart because of a single, desperate mistake. I forced my breathing to steady, pushing the bloodlust down, hiding the chaos from the paladin at my side.

Suddenly, chaos crashed through my thoughts into reality. Horses thundered past, arrows fell from the trees, shouts of "AMBUSH!" erupted. The mystics reacted instantly, raising a barrier of stone. Megan fled, missing the real threat ahead. I lunged, tackled her clear of a blade, taking a graze to my arm.

"Are you alright?" I asked as I caught my breath. She nodded, shaken.

The battle was fierce—flames leaped up trees, water crashed down on the bandits. The mystics finished the attackers quickly, but Rostov was nowhere to be seen. I ordered Darion to douse the flames. We didn't need to torch the cursed forest on top of everything else.

We broke camp sooner than planned and made for Sylhalin. Megan and her mystics split off for Sarnawen; I pressed on with Darion. The silence between us grew heavy. My thoughts drifted again to Akira—the threat she posed, the temptation to end things once and for all. It was like poison, an itch beneath my skin, but I held myself in check.

Sylhalin finally rose on the horizon. Up ahead, I saw Akira walking, Atlas the cub trotting on a rope at her side. My composure nearly cracked. I could end it here, draw my sword, and rid the world of her chaos. But I kept my hand off the hilt. I had to play the king, not the executioner—at least not yet.

As I approached the gates alone, the men on the wall rushed to open them. What awaited was a nightmare: my soldiers, kneeling with their hands on their heads, Rostov behind them, sword raised and that wicked smile painted across his face.

"Welcome to New Zodan! Business or pleasure?" Rostov shouted, his eyes full of glee. "*Let the festivities begin.*"

Chapter 13: A very lucky opportunity.

The remaining members of my group were given a choice: surrender or death. We all ended up kneeling in shackles. Akira, as usual, was reluctant—she stayed standing, it sickened me.

She could never just follow instructions; she readied her sword in hand. Soldiers began circling her and the cub. Atlas bared his fangs and pounced on the first one, grabbing him by the neck and thrashing him around.

Akira pulled her sword and followed his lead. Just as she charged at Rostov, he pulled out an odd object, pointed it to the sky, and fired. The echo split the silence, stopping Akira just before her sword touched his neck. He turned the weapon on her face.

"Drop your weapon," Rostov ordered.

She stayed still, her cub still feasting on soldiers. Rostov aimed at the cub. "*Now.*"

Akira's face twitched beneath her scarf; her eyes narrowed—but finally, she complied. She dropped the sword and knelt in front of him.

Rostov smiled and let out a laugh. "You like it? Got it from some dark elf outside my castle—tinkers with machines. *Virmath* calls this a 'flintlock revolver.' I like it better than the sword. People listen more." He waved it around before holstering it on his hip. My spine shuddered at the name, my former ally aiding my rival. *Disgusting.*

Rostov bent down and tugged down Akira's scarf, his thumb brushing a mark on her cheek. "We really must stop meeting like this," he teased, his eyes flicking to the cub. Atlas had stopped attacking and now sat beside Akira, growling at Rostov's every move.

"Remember what happened last time?" he continued. "You hunted my prey. I wouldn't have been as mad if you hadn't pitied it—refusing to kill something in pain is inhumane. That's what makes you weak." He sneered.

His tone rose with each word. Akira's scowl deepened, her breath growing heavier. Halfway through his rant, she lunged—kneeing him in the stomach.

"HOW'S THAT FOR WEAK!?" she shouted, grabbing her sword and holding it, shackled hands and all, to his throat.

Rostov cackled, still catching his breath. "I knew you had some fight in you. You have greatness—the perfect prey. Even in a losing battle, you don't back down." His voice was hoarse, but not without admiration.

"Atlas and I aren't with them or the city," Akira said. "You can have them. But we're leaving." She nodded toward me and the others. She whistled; Atlas circled behind her, still snarling. She kept her blade at Rostov's neck.

He smiled, then nodded. "No better hunt than catch and release." He glanced at a soldier. "Unshackle her." He barked at his men.

The cuffs hit the dirt. Akira backed away slowly. The gate rose—and with a slam, she and the cub disappeared from the city.

Rostov stood up with a sigh. "Take them to the cells. The exciting two are gone." He waved off my group, and his men herded us away.

As we were led through Sylhalin, I watched the city burn—its streets no longer gleaming, buildings ransacked or destroyed. Citizens stared as we passed. The observatory was being refitted in grim gray stone. The city had become a shell of itself. Hanging from one of the posts outside the observatory was Eldric, or what was left of him.

They dragged us into a basement lined with cells. One by one, we were thrown in separately. I leaned against my wall and stared out into the corridor.

Sam's figure appeared—sitting cross-legged on my cot, hands in his lap. He looked at me, disappointed.

I rolled my eyes. “I know. I should’ve fought. But I can't do much from here, I’m so tired, Sam.” I sighed deeply.

Sam managed a small, reassuring smile. Even dead, he gave me confidence. But that smile couldn’t change what happened.

He’d still be alive if it weren’t for *Akira*. Did Sam knocking out Drake really justify what she did? Three people died because I trusted her. Because I let my guard down. No. This wasn’t survival. It was *murder.*

As I brooded, Sam turned his head toward the stairs. He stood, walked through the bars, then vanished.

Footsteps echoed. I strained to see who approached.

A woman in a red dress dashed down the stairs. Dark skin, dreadlocks streaked with color, sharp eyes—she didn’t look like anyone from Rhova. She stopped at my cell, pulled out a key, and unlocked the door.

“You coming?” she asked. Her accent was lilting, her tone impatient.

For a moment I just stared. She raised an eyebrow, and I snapped out of it, following her toward the exit—then stopped.

"What are you doing?" she hissed.

"I need the key," I said, hand out. She passed it over, and I sprinted back, unlocking cells for my followers. When everyone was free, I tossed the key and rejoined her.

We reached the street. I paused. "I need a weapon," I said.

She grabbed my wrist. "No. We're leaving."

"I can't leave," I said. "I have to reclaim the spectre." I said urgently, she rolled her eyes.

"I didn't free you to get recaptured on a half-baked plan," she snapped. I stared—her voice, her presence.

She caught my look and snapped her fingers. "My eyes are up here."

I mumbled an apology.

"I need the observatory," I said. "Without it, I have nothing."

She sighed. "You think I came here by accident? Queen Cilmair wants a word. And she can't do that if you're tortured or dead."

My mind spun. Queen Cilmair—a powerful priestess, crowned Queen of Lolem, but *Why me?*

"*Fine,*" I said. "But we meet in Eîthor. She can choose the time, but I choose the place."

She nodded hesitantly.

"Wait," she called. "Cilmair won't be happy to hear I returned empty handed."

I shook my head. "Just tell Cilmair to meet me in Eîthor. She'll know why." I paused. "Your name?"

"Priya," she said.

"Pleasure," I replied—and slipped back into the city.

Not for long. The hunt has just begun.

I'm not done here. Not until I take back my city. Not until Rostov regrets underestimating me. And for bait?

Akira.

Chapter 14: A Pleasant Surprise

I sat at a cliffside watching Sylhalin burn in the distance. My eyes fell to the campfire I had built just low enough not to draw attention from anyone nearby. Atlas tossed and turned in his sleep, letting out little low growls. I reached over and began to pet him. He crawled over and lay down on my lap, and I leaned back against a tree. I sat there listening to Atlas' breathing—it was almost soothing. I began to feel a weight, an exhaustion I didn't think I could hold off anymore.

I glanced down at Atlas, my hand still petting him. I closed my eyes and drifted off to sleep. I dreamt about a lot of things, reminiscing about the life I had lived, my regrets, those I have come to love, and those I will miss until the day I die. My surroundings seemed familiar—it was my childhood home. I walked inside to see my mom wearing an apron and chopping vegetables. She looked up from what she was doing and gave me a giant smile.

"Akira, you're back!" she said, spreading her arms before rushing to hug me. The feeling of her arms around me made me want to collapse and never let go. Her tears slipped down her cheeks, but her smile was bright and whole, just like it always was before everything changed.

"I missed you, Mama," I whispered, trying to keep my voice steady.

She wiped her cheeks, still grinning. “I always knew you’d come home, even if just for a little while.”

We sat at the table together, sharing dinner like we did in the days when the world was smaller and kinder. I tried to push the sadness away, but it lingered, heavy in my chest. She told a joke about the neighbor’s goose chasing her in the garden, and I laughed, for a moment forgetting the ache inside me.

Then, gently, she squeezed my hands. “Akira, love is not a safe thing. It will leave you *raw*, but it is the only thing that makes us brave enough to face the world. Do you remember when you were small and climbed the old oak, even though you were afraid? I stood under the branches and told you: If you fall, I’ll catch you. I still will, if you need me to.”

I blinked away tears, holding on to the feeling of her warm hands, the echo of her laugh.

“But I don’t know how to let myself love again,” I confessed.

She brushed my hair back from my forehead, just like she used to, and looked at me with soft eyes. “You don’t have to know how, Akira. You just must want to try. That’s enough.”

Her smile faded, becoming gentle and distant as a commotion outside the house arose. "It's time for you to go," she said, nodding to the doorway, the sky beyond growing brighter. "Remember, you carry my love with you, wherever you are. And if you ever need to fall, I'll catch you."

I tried to say, "I miss you," but the dream was already slipping away. She stood by the window, waving, and for a moment she looked as young as I remembered her—before the world went to war.

Her voice lingered as I woke: "Go. He needs you." The dream ended with my distant screams *"NOOOO! MAMA!!!! NO!"* the sound of my own pleas reverberated in my ears.

I awoke with a start and rose to my feet; the fire had died. The stars lit up the sky, and the fires of Sylhalin were still burning bright. I rubbed Atlas behind the ears, and he let out a yawn. I crouched there, leaning up against the tree, trying to figure out my next step. While I was deep in thought, Atlas stopped licking himself. He turned his attention to the only path off the cliff. Atlas took a defensive stance and bared his fangs, letting out a spine-tingling roar.

I grabbed my katana and stood behind Atlas. I didn't see or hear anything, but he only got more defensive. I grabbed my gear and slowly headed down the path, Atlas leading the way. Once we reached the bottom of the cliff path, he calmed. The sun slowly began to rise filling the sky with a light pink hue, and Atlas and I started heading back toward Sylhalin. I had a hunch that Drake needed me, and I didn't know why, but I was drawn to the city yet again.

We walked in silence for a while. I thought about my mom, and how it had almost been a decade since the imperials raided my village. I thought about being shoved in a wagon and watching my mother fight to get to me, getting executed in the center of town. My heart sank; I fell to the ground. Atlas stopped and turned back to check why I'd stopped. I wiped my face and rubbed his head. I just needed a minute. The time passed but the grief hasn't dulled.

I sat on the dirt path in the middle of nowhere, I noticed something in the road up ahead, Atlas circling around me, watching in every direction. I stifled some sobs and continued to check it out. Atlas and I approached a corpse in the road, I examined the dead man closely, *I'd seen him before*, he was the other paladin in Verath's company, *Darion.* Intrigued, I examined him further, he had bruises around his neck like he was strangled. I wasn't sure how long ago, but his skin had begun to turn purple and pale white in some spots, and he was beginning to smell, just as I was about to move him out of the road, there was a clattering down the path. I looked in both directions and saw a wagon being pulled by two horses. I quickly gathered my things and whistled to Atlas. I ran off the path and toward the forest; when they saw Atlas and me, they only sped up, turning off the path and following us in full-speed pursuit.

Atlas and I ran into the forest and turned randomly until we reached a climbable tree toward the center. We climbed up and observed. Six men got out of the wagon, armed with odd weapons about the length of a sword, but they held them to their faces and used both hands. I watched them spread out, fanning out in search of us.

The remaining men in my view searched behind every tree. They eventually regrouped ahead of my tree. I couldn't see them, but I could hear them.

One man was shouting to the rest: "HOW COULD SHE JUST DISAPPEAR? SHE HAD A TIGER!" There was a sudden sound like an explosion, and then a man flew back, slamming into a tree. He began to bleed, his head falling to his chest. "Quiet, you'll spook her, Boss wants her alive."

I let out a *gasp*. What were these men using? What could possibly throw a man into a tree and *kill him*? Atlas lay further down my branch, licking his paws and flicking his tail, as if this were just another morning. He turned his attention toward the sound of the man's yelling.

The men split up again. One man came to the base of my tree, looked up, and aimed his weapon at me. He let out a shout, but before he could fire, Atlas pounced and tore into his throat. The man's eyes widened as he stared into mine, Atlas snapping his neck and ending him.

My spine tingled. I was once again grateful that Atlas was on my side. I hopped down out of the tree, pulled out my katana, and watched Atlas drag his kill up a tree, his little body struggling with the weight, but succeeding, He's not quite grown, but his instincts are true.

Two of the six men were dead; four remained. I stuck to the shadows, ready to slash anything that appeared. I took cover in some bushes and watched two men patrolling together. One had his weapon on his back, the other was ready for anything, aiming around almost in a paranoid way.

The men began to argue. "You should take our job seriously. You know we'll get paid more if we capture them alive."

The lazy one scoffed. "They disappeared once. If they can do it again, what's the point?" He wandered off.

I slowly approached the eager man. I was about to slash my sword when the other man approached again, looked at me with wide eyes, and dropped his canteen. The man in front of me turned and fired his weapon, but missed, hitting a tree. I reacted, slitting his throat, and held my blade to the lazy man's throat, grabbing him and holding him in front of me defensively.

The remaining men ran toward us, one in full armor, head to toe. He gave a chuckle which echoed thanks to his helmet. He clapped his hands. "You have *quite* the bounty on your head," he said, pulling out a wanted poster with my face.

I pressed my katana to the man's throat and dragged; he started to bleed. The armored man made a sound I couldn't decipher, pulled out a flintlock, and shot the man next to him. The man's corpse fell. The man I was holding continued to squirm; the armored man shot the last of his own men. The man I was holding collapsed to the ground in front of me, the armored man then aimed at me. "Drop the sword," he ordered sternly.

I stood there, cornered. I couldn't cut him through his armor, Atlas was preoccupied, and he could shoot me if I ran. I tried to think of a way out, but nothing came to mind. I dropped the sword as ordered and ducked. He fired into the tree behind me.

I rolled behind him and swept his leg; he fell to the ground with a grunt. I kicked his weapon away, ripped off his helmet, and kicked it aside. I picked up my katana and held it to his face while I held him down. The man's face was scarred, his eyes dark. He yanked a fistful of my hair, throwing me off him. I stumbled backward and hit a tree, my head spinning.

The man got up, grabbed his flintlock, and approached me.

“You shouldn’t have fought; you had me at your mercy, and you *failed.* Why even weaken my defense if you weren’t going to try?” He held the weapon to my face.

I stared into his eyes and lowered my scarf to my chin.

“I didn’t do it for me.” I took a breath and let out a whistle that cut through the chilly morning air. The man’s face went dark when Atlas let out a roar. The man panicked, fired three random shots, and then dove for his helmet. Atlas pounced, jaws bloody, as the man dropped his weapon Now, he stared into Atlas’s teeth.

I stood up and whistled. Atlas backed up and looked to me. I walked to the man and yanked the wanted poster from his hand. I unrolled it and read the description.

‘Akira of Khofte, 5ft 5, dark hair, light skin, wields a sword, last seen in the Sarnawenian Forests probably accompanied by a man and a medium-sized tiger. Price when returned to New Zodan alive: 48,000 gold pieces. Price for all corpses: 15,000 silver pieces.’

I scoffed. *"Rostov."* I crumpled the paper and threw it to the ground. I approached the man, still hyperventilating by the tree. I swung my katana over and held it to the bottom of his chin, lifting until he looked up at me with tearful eyes.

"I need to get into New Zodan, but not as a prisoner. You *will* get me in there."

The man shook his head, "*...No.*" he whimpered.

I released my blade and let Atlas approach.

"YES! YES! OKAY…! I'LL GET YOU IN, JUST DON'T KILL ME!" he sobbed.

I called off Atlas, grabbed the weapons off the corpses, and carried them to the wagon. I left the prisoner under Atlas' watch, waved him over, and whistled to Atlas. They both boarded the wagon. Atlas claimed a spot in the back; the man climbed up front.

I held my sword to his neck as he grabbed the reins. "Pull *anything* funny and I won't hesitate next time," I said, dragging the blade just enough to make him bleed a little. He gripped his neck and nodded fearfully as I removed my sword.

I climbed in the wagon next to Atlas and rubbed his head. The wagon burst to life and the war-torn forest slowly shrank behind the horizon.

I let out a sigh, "*I'm coming, Drake.*"

As the wagon jolted along the road, I caught a fleeting memory—Drake and I, back at the fire on our second night of uneasy truce, when he had just finished telling a story so ridiculous we both laughed until we were out of breath. He had managed to coax a smile out of me, even then, and in that moment, it had felt possible that the world could be warm again.

I clung to that memory now, letting it light something inside me, even as the path ahead darkened in Sylhalin's dying shadow.

Chapter 15: Passing the Time

I sat and watched the sun rise through the thin crack in the wagon's fabric. Using a ceramic jug of water, I quickly rinsed my hair—it had been a while since I bathed, and it couldn't hurt. Atlas had fallen asleep on the floor near my feet, looking so peaceful I couldn't help but rest my hand on his head for a moment, feeling the slow rhythm of his breath. I searched for a bowl or saucer to give him some water, shaking out my travel-worn pack with one hand.

I opened the front wagon flap and startled the man leading the horses.

"Oh, *calm down*. I just need your helmet," I said with a sigh I didn't know I was holding.

The man looked like he wanted to protest but was too scared to try. I grabbed his helmet, filled it as much as I could with water, and lowered it in front of Atlas. The cub lifted his head, *unimpressed* with a bowl that smelled faintly of facial sweat but eventually drank from it. I set the helmet down, then sat on the bench and pressed my fingers into my eyes for a second, grounding myself.

"How much longer until we reach the city?" I asked the man.

"Uh… a few hours if we keep this pace. It's usually a day or two on foot. This is faster," he replied.

I nodded, reached into my pack, and pulled out the leather-bound diary. I lay back and disappeared into someone else's story for a while.

The entries were by a mother named Theresa. She wrote about her daughter, Mixa, and how life had once been happy—until Rotík's rise to tyranny. The mystics of the village panicked, enforcing limits, curfews, mandates. I paused at the word *mandates*, feeling my jaw tense. I could almost smell the smoke of my childhood home and hear the boots outside the door.

The elders had ordered a *"last resort"* for all villagers. Theresa didn't explain what it was. As I read, my thumb rubbed the edge of the page, catching on a splotch—maybe a tear stain? My heart twisted, thinking of all the things mothers never get to say.

"The elders of the village have mandated that all mystics who can use their powers effectively in combat are to be fitted for armor and sent on our first scouting mission outside the forest. I protested, but they didn't listen. I don't want to leave Mixa, but they threatened to exile us. 'Let them take us,' were the elders' exact words."

I had to stop and flex my fingers, my nails leaving small crescents in my palm. I blinked back the sting in my eyes and read on.

The next entry was different.

"The scouting mission went off without a hitch. It was amazing—I was able to use my abilities in the real world, not just in a bucket in the village. It was invigorating. We gathered information about the nearest imperial camp and their next moves. It was oddly empty; we slipped in and out without alerting the patrolling soldiers.

But when we returned... destruction. Soldiers killing mystics and vice versa. My heart sank. MIXA.

I ran toward our house on the northern edge of the village, dodging and fighting to get there. I threw open the door—just her stuffed bear on the floor. I searched every room and came up empty. I could barely breathe. Where would the elders take her?

I ran out the door and bumped into a man—brown hair, scout's armor, longsword on his back. He apologized, but I didn't hear him. It was just Drake. I shook it off and ran toward the center of the village. I'll find you, Mixa. I promise."

I swallowed, rereading the line about the stuffed bear. I remembered Drake's voice— *"I knew the girl who had this bear, long ago."*

I closed my eyes, trying to picture that lost child holding onto a scrap of comfort in a burning world.

I looked up from the diary. Atlas lay with his head poking out of the flap, watching the scenery go by. I popped through the front flap to check with the man.

“An hour, tops,” he said, looking bored. “We’re close.”

I lay back down and kept reading. My thumb smoothed the page as I turned it.

The next entry felt out of place, but I read anyway.

“The elders have begun the last resort protocol. The curfew is stricter now. Council members guard our doors. Some houses are still burning, and they’re keeping people locked inside. It’s inhumane!

I’m writing this by candlelight with a guard staring at me. They’ve taken the children. They won’t tell me where Mixa is. I fought and pleaded—they refused to let me see her. They’ll be releasing the children from the southern side of the village…”

I let the diary rest open on my lap and stared at the wagon ceiling.

Why were the mystics targeted? What was the last resort? My mind returned to the night I found Drake—encased in a tree, *wild* and *violent*, but not in his heart. Just before Rostov captured him, he’d created a wall of flame—hot enough to sear. He's a mystic, but not a half-breed. He's *ancient.*

They're all dead… *right?*

I pressed the diary to my chest. My pulse thudded in my ears.

I needed answers.

I placed the book back in my pack and rubbed Atlas behind the ears. My eyes drifted to the pile of weapons I'd looted from the bounty hunters. I picked up a flintlock and examined it carefully. It worked like a crossbow would, launching a projectile—the spark, the gunpowder, the release. A chain reaction.

I popped up front. "Stop the wagon." I ordered.

"Why?" the man asked, confused.

I hopped out with the flintlock. He followed me around to the side as I inspected the weapons. Without me saying more, he began to speak.

"This is a flintlock revolver. Five shots, then you reload," he said.

"I figured that out already," I replied unimpressed.

He chuckled and clapped cockily. “Try it then.”

I raised the weapon and fired two clean shots at a nearby tree. Smoke drifted from the barrel. The man clapped again, slower this time.

“Beginner’s luck.”

He tried to take the weapon. I stepped back and drew it on him.

“Remember *earlier?*” I hissed. “Remember how you *couldn’t* catch me? How I spared you?”

I pressed the barrel to his chin. “Don’t man up now. I’m just getting started.” The man flinched as if my words had bit him.

I took the ammo and strapped the flintlock holster around my waist.

Back in the wagon, Atlas snoozed. I asked the man, “What’s your name?”

“Zeke,” he muttered, eyes forward.

Unimpressed, I returned to the bench—until we suddenly stopped.

I heard a voice outside.

"---*check the back.*"

I drew my katana. As the flap lifted, Zeke tackled the guard and beat him savagely.

I gasped. "My god."

I held Atlas back. "You're not coming with me. This city's too dangerous. I'll be back."

Atlas growled low, but gave a final shake of the head, and he lied down.

I turned to Zeke, stone-faced.

"If you hurt him, I'll end you," I said, grabbing his chin. "He's not defenseless."

Atlas growled again. Zeke backed away from the wagon.

I pulled up my scarf and made for the gate. No cover, no entry—unless they let me in.

A wagon approached. I leapt aboard and opened a chest—*fruitcake,* and *gold.* I took the gold, then pulled some folded fabric over my head and used a chain to clasp it at my neck.

The gate rose to life. The wagon rolled in. I waited, then—

Now!

I rolled off, landing in front of what used to be the Sylhalin observatory.

Everything was grim. Buildings crumbled. Flames burned on, blackening the air. Ragged people stumbled through the streets, some bearing scars like open wounds.

My spine prickled.

What the hell happened here?

Chapter 16: A light change of attitude, Nevermind.

I wandered the streets of the city that was once Sylhalin. The crowds were thick and restless, new ruler, new colors, but it still felt like a powder keg. My mind wandered, thinking of all that could still go wrong—how little it would take for my fragile order to snap. I couldn't return to Ciron without having a foothold in this continent, and everything seemed to be going wrong.

That was when I caught a glimpse of a face in the crowd. Brown hair tattered white shirt, and a staff in hand. For a heartbeat, I thought I was seeing things. But the familiarity stuck with me. *Drake?* It couldn't be. Still, I felt myself drawn forward, weaving through strangers, the pressure in my chest rising as I hurried not to lose him.

He slipped into a building, and my gut told me to follow. I glanced around, ducked inside, and caught the door before it shut. The place was dim, crowded with dust and shadows. I crept through a side hallway, found a letter opener on a desk, and slipped it into my hand—*just in case.*

I turned a corner and spotted the man from before, just about to disappear into a back room. Instinct took over. I grabbed him, pressing the letter opener to his throat before he could react.

"Hello there, Drake," I said, keeping my voice low, trying to mask the adrenaline. "Searching for *something?"*

Drake tensed and tried to wriggle free. "You seemed so nice when we met. What's *changed?*" I asked, letting a bit of old sarcasm slip in.

He shot back, "The blade kind of dampens the mood, don't you think?" His eyes were sharp, he was off, I could *sense* it.

I eased the pressure but didn't let go. My mind kept racing, counting all the things that could go wrong—another public scene, another complication. I spotted shackles on the desk, snapped them on his wrists, and kept him close.

"Let's go. *Out*." I ordered, tugging him outside and into the busy street. My grip was tight, and every sideways glance from passersby felt like another nail in the coffin of my *so-called* control.

Drake tried to keep his composure. "Aren't you going to ask why I'm in your city?" he asked, as if he had something to prove.

"Nope," I said, forcing some levity. "Didn't you hear? Not my city as of a few hours ago. But I'll ask when it is." I almost smiled at the shock on his face. We made our way to the southern gate and then into the valley, toward the only stronghold I still had left, Eîthor.

We walked through the wild grass and up toward the castle. "Why are we here?" Drake asked, a bitter edge in his voice. He wasn't his usual self—less bright, more wary and hostile.

I told him the truth, or at least enough of it: I'd keep him here to draw out Akira, then use her to get Rostov, and finally take back the city. Another desperate plan, one more gamble. I could feel my pulse in my throat.

Once we arrived, I marched him to the cells and ordered the guards to keep him alive—but not to open the gate for anyone. Drake just went in, no protest. No fight left in him. I didn't stop to think about how it made me feel.

Upstairs in my chambers, I tried to shed the tension with my uniform. There was never any real peace. A knock at the door broke my reverie. A servant entered, "There is a woman here for you, sir." He stated, I nodded and dressed quickly and went down.

Megan was waiting—glasses, red hair pinned back, nose already buried in a book. "Sir, it's a pleasure to see you again," she said. I nodded and led her to the library, the familiar dread returning—too many secrets, too many knives waiting in the dark.

She spoke eagerly. “I think that Rotik’s heiress resides in Sarnawen.” I nodded. “You said this last time.” I said sternly. She shook her head, “That was hypothetical. This is a real lead. The Queen who rules Sarnawen hasn’t shown her face. She’s only known by name—*Camilla*”

I felt my patience fray. “I need more than a guess,” I told her, but inside I wondered if any of these leads ever mattered. Megan’s face lit up at the tiniest scrap of approval. “We can investigate further tomorrow!” she gushed. A servant brought drinks; I downed mine to steady my nerves. Megan fumbled, dropped her tome, and rushed towards the door, “sir…?” she asked softly, I turned towards her, “Have you seen Darion since your return? You were the last person seen with him, before we parted ways.” she asked meekly, her earlier excitement lost in her suspicions, “What are you accusing me of Megan?” I asked firmly. “Nothing, sir!” she said as vanished from the room in a rush.

I stood at the window, bourbon in hand, city lights glittering beneath the dark sky. It should have felt like victory. Instead, every second felt like I was waiting for disaster. Years of fighting, of outmaneuvering tyrants like Roldan, and the world always seemed one misstep away from collapse.

A sharp rap at the door. “My lord, apologies, you have a visi—” A woman swept in before the servant could finish, knocking him to the floor. “*Pathetic,*” she muttered, tossing her hat onto the poor man. He struggled to his feet. "Queen Cilmair, at your service," he spat, then scurried off.

Cilmair took my hand with calculated grace, dropped her cloak for a servant to fetch, and sat at the table, already sneering at my décor. "Why must we meet in this *dreadful* place instead of my garden?" she demanded. I kept my expression neutral. "We both *know* why. Let's not pretend we haven't both done our research." I said politely.

She snapped her fingers, trying to summon some unseen aid. Nothing happened. With a growl, she stormed to the door and shrieked for her lackey, who rushed in and handed her a scroll. She tossed it to me. The message was clear: plans to rally the Light royals against Eîthor, to "purify" the land.

She made her pitch—Lolem will help me take the continent, she remains the royal, I get my war, and she keeps her power. Her words were honeyed, but I heard the venom underneath.

She stepped close, fingers tracing my jaw, then tightening on my neck. "Think about it," she purred sweetly as she moved to the door.

I hurled my glass past her head. "Choose your tone *wisely*. Next time, I won't miss." I said with a forced smile. She grumbled and slipped out. Her shrill yell for her servant echoed down the corridor.

I slumped in my chair, fear and anger circling like vultures. Had I just made a deal with the very thing I was supposed to be fighting?

I left the library, notified a servant about the broken glass, and descended to the dungeon. Laughter and chatter from the guards grated on my last nerves. I cut through it, took the key, opened Drake's cell, and barked, "*LET'S GO.*"

He shuffled out, arms shackled. "Where are you taking me *now*?" I ignored the bite in his voice and brought him to the dining hall, freeing his wrists. He looked at me, surprised, then rubbed at the red marks.

A servant brought food, and Drake devoured it, barely pausing to breathe. I watched, uneasy, the room growing quieter with every passing second.

After his sixth mutton-chop, Drake finally spoke, voice quiet:
"I… I… Did something *horrible*… but there was a waterfall southwest of the city—we got *separated.* When I woke up, I was *cold*, *alone*, and my head was bleeding. I thought *maybe* she'd follow the path like I did. I didn't know what else to do. I *don't* deserve to find her, but I feel I should, *something* told me to try."

He let out a short, bitter laugh. “Guess wandering into hell counts as doing something, didn’t think that Sylhalin would be mid civil war. Why are you being so nice to me? I certainly don't deserve it.” He asked mostly in one breath mid-chew.

I hesitated. *Was* it for the plan—to draw *Akira out?* —or because I was tired of watching people get hurt for no reason? I settled for the easy answer: “I need you in one piece to lure Akira. That’s all.” I said sternly.

He grinned, mouth full, and gave me a slow but steady hug. I grunted and shoved him off, but his arms tightened before letting go. Not out of desperation—but meaning. I caught the shake in his breath as he backed away.

Even shattered, he still had enough heart to care.

As I walked away, I realized the fear hadn’t left me. I was still one heartbeat away from losing control, and *I knew it*.

Chapter 17: A Glance into the Future to be

I stood in front of what was once the observatory of Sylhalin, astounded by every stubborn sign of life. I secured my coverings and moved toward what passed for a makeshift bazaar. Dirt-stained bricks made up the paths, and people turned to look as I passed—*me,* the outsider.

I stopped at a tent lined with odd wares: dragon scale, rabbit's foot, and trinkets with no real use for someone like me. My eyes landed on a shimmering orb. Each glance made it dance with color. The woman behind the counter noticed. She glided forward, voice warm but practiced. "Interested in the looking glass?" she asked.

"What can you tell me about it?" I kept my tone casual.

She lifted the orb with ceremony. "This looking glass glimpses the near future. It senses your motions, shows you your path—adventurers who've lost their way come to it." She sounded like she was selling magic beans. I was almost drawn in. But when I reached out to touch the orb, she slapped my hand away.

"Only the pure-willed may gaze into the glass." Her tone went hollow, eyes unblinking. "I can look for you, for a price—and a grasp of the hand, my dear." Before I could protest, she seized my hand, placed a sheet between us and the orb, and closed her eyes.

Her grip only tightened. I tried to pull back, but she held my arm firmly. She opened her eyes—and suddenly, the bazaar seemed to vanish into fog.

"You have the heart of a warrior, but the lust for vengeance." Her voice changed—softer now. She turned back to the orb, brow furrowed, then gasped.

Facing me again, she took my other hand. "You've felt heartbreak—more than most. That pain has sent you down a *dark* path. But it makes you stronger than the rest. You are a warrior filled with *rage*. Though misery follows you, you carry a torch others are drawn to, some who are drawn are dangerous, *jealous, s*eeking to extinguish you."

Her hands trembled around mine.

She touched the orb again. Eyes shut, her face tensed. Then—she exhaled. "You've begun to evolve. You've broken a cycle of anguish and found a fondness for someone new."

I was tense. My jaw locked in place; I yearned to move but she was stubborn.

"Your path intertwines with an *ancient legacy*—one that could shape the fate of Rhova." She lifted my chin. "You must choose wisely. Your past is not a burden. It's an edge. Very few have lived through what you have. You've earned strength, instinct, and have an undying loyalty to those who prove themselves. You don't just stand for yourself anymore. You stand for the innocent."

She let go, covered the orb, and stepped back. *Innocent*, my mind flashed with Atlas and Drake in Rostov's clutches. I clenched my teeth. The woman's eyes narrowed, "Yes… *Them*, you'll protect them. And *more*." She said in a harrowed tone.

I took a breath. My past as an edge? My advantage? I left the small pouch of gold on the table and thanked her. She nodded and slipped behind a curtain.

I moved on. The crowd thinned. I asked after Drake—most ignored me, but one woman muttered she saw someone like him by the southern gate. When I pressed, she turned away.

I turned back toward the observatory. It was slowly being cased in gray concrete. Rebuilding. At least one building was being built. Most of Sylhalin was still wreckage, but a few homes stood defiant.

My thoughts drifted to Drake. The last time I saw him, he ran. *Haunted. Guilty.* Still out there, hurting.

I looked for signs of order. Nothing. Just wreckage. I reached what was left of the prison. Desks toppled, blood on the walls. No bodies. The cells were empty.

"Hey!" a voice barked.

I turned to a ragged man. Greasy hair. Flintlock at his belt. He drew it, but I kicked him in the chest before he could even think about firing. He hit the ground.

I stepped on his neck. "Did you *need* something?" He struggled, face red. I let go and crouched beside him.

"Next time you pick a fight, think *twice*. You don't want to know what I do to people who get in my way. Be grateful, I'm in a *hurry*." I let him run off. I had bigger problems.

I lingered, then circled back toward the observatory. A crowd was forming at the doors—shouting, pushing, desperate.

Then—three cannon shots exploded into the crowd.

Bodies dropped. Screaming. Trampling. Rostov appeared, flanked by bandits, picking off survivors with his flintlock.

He saw me.
He fired.
I dove into an alley and ran. *FUCK.*

Chapter 18: Protecting those in need

I ran through the narrow alleys, dodging wild gunfire. I ducked and swerved, trying to be a difficult target. Another shot cracked the air—Rostov had fired again. Pain continued to tear through my arm. Radiating to my fingertips.

He fucking shot me.

What is wrong with him?

Still clutching the wound, I kept running, breath shallow and vision blurring. I turned a corner, then another, and collapsed into a doorway, crouching low. My heartbeat pounded in my ears as I tried to steady my breathing. In the distance, I heard Rostov shout, "Find her—*NOW!*"

Footsteps thundered past my hiding spot.

I risked a glance at my arm. Blood was pouring out, but the bullet had gone clean through. I ripped a piece of my ratty cloak and wrapped it tightly around the wound. When I stood, I saw the trail of blood I'd left behind.

Shit. I needed to move—*now*.

I crept out into the street and found myself near the southern gates of the city. I thought about leaving Sylhalin altogether, but gunfire cracked a few blocks away.

Screams followed. Rostov had lost his mind. He was just killing people now—no reason, no mercy.

I wanted to search for Drake, but I had no leads, no direction, nothing to go on. So, I turned to the gates leading to Eîthor. From here, I could see its lights glowing faintly in the distance. I pressed my hand to the cool metal bars.

Locked. Of course.

I stepped back, scanning for another way out. The city was on lockdown—trying to keep people in. I sighed. I couldn't stay here. Not with Rostov out there, prowling the streets.

"Psst."

I froze.

"PSSST."

I turned to a nearby alley and approached cautiously. A boy stood half-hidden in the shadows. "Looking for a way out?" he asked quietly. I nodded. He gestured for me to follow and walked briskly toward the curve of the southern wall. I trailed behind him, wary.

We reached a house nestled into the corner where the east and south walls met. He pulled out a wooden ladder.

He propped it up against the side of the house and climbed to the roof with practiced ease. He waved for me to follow. I hesitated, then climbed up after him.

Now I understood—this section of the wall was lower, the ground sloping sharply in a way that made the jump feasible. He laid the ladder across the gap between the rooftop and wall and carefully crossed.

I followed.

Once we were both on the other side, he dropped the ladder and led me to the edge. The drop was maybe fifteen or twenty feet to Eîthorian soil—not as bad as I feared. I knelt beside him. “Thank you,” I said.

He smiled, then leapt. I followed with a roll, landing hard but steady. We both took off in opposite directions. I headed toward the dockside houses up ahead.

After about a half hour of walking, I reached the outskirts of the port district. I froze.

Why am I even here?

Drake might not even be nearby. I had no proof, no trail. But before I could turn back towards Sylhalin, I heard music—*cheering*. Curious, I moved toward the sound and found a crowded tavern.

I slipped inside, just as a man near the door cheered, “We’re waiting for an encore! The singer was incredible!”

I glanced at the stage. A woman stepped forward: dark skin, shoulder-length dreadlocks woven with beads, a red dress slit in the front. Her presence was commanding. She didn't fit the mold of anyone on Rhova. She smiled nervously, took a breath—and began to sing.

The song had no words, just a melody that was aching, haunting. As she sang, tears slipped down her face. The emotion in her voice made my chest tighten. When the last note faded, she bowed gracefully and wiped her cheeks.

“Thank you,” she said with an accent I didn’t recognize. “I’m late for a meeting, but it was an honor to perform for you all.”

She disappeared behind the curtain. The crowd groaned in disappointment.

I ordered a whiskey and sat at the bar. The room stayed lively, but smaller clusters formed. A group of men nearby talked about conspiracies and rumors.

“Sarnawen’s planning a siege on Zodan and Sylhalin,” one muttered, “Sarnawen may just take out Lolem too just for allying with Verath.”

"They want the countryside back," another agreed.

I kept my hood low, listening. The men moved to a table, and I followed, using the crowd for cover.

"I heard Lolem is defecting to Lord Verath's side," one man said. "Queen Cilmair was spotted leaving the Eîthorian keep."

"Verath has a prisoner," another added. "First I've seen since his return."

My pulse quickened. Could he have found the Heiress he was seeking?

I leaned closer, but just as they started to speak again, a loud horn blared from outside. The tavern shifted. People began pouring out. As I turned to follow, one of the men I'd been eavesdropping on caught my arm.

"You alright?" he asked with a grin.

I pulled my arm free.

"If you'd been more subtle, I might've spilled a little more," he teased with a wink, before walking off.

Outside, another horn blew—closer this time. The gates to Sylhalin groaned open, and rows of soldiers marched through into the valley of Eîthor, the crowd panicked.

A siege.

I stood still, heart thudding. I could run into the city, search for Drake while the streets cleared—but the oracle's voice echoed in my mind:

"You do not stand for yourself anymore. You stand for the *innocent.*"

I took off my cloak and drew my katana.

And turned to the terrified crowd behind me.

"EVERYONE! IN YOUR HOUSES! BARRICADE YOUR DOORS—NOW!" I ordered.

The soldiers split, some heading for Verath's castle, others toward the port. I stood alone on the hill as they descended.

Over my dead body.

Chapter 19: The End of the Hunt

The armies marched toward the town and the castle of Eîthor. I stood, katana in hand, waiting for them to come to me. When they drew close, it was clear—they weren't traditional soldiers. Ragged clothes, poor hygiene, but moving like an army. They stopped about twenty feet away, the line of weapons glinting in the morning light.

Each man raised his weapon—muskets, all of them. One shot from each could rip me in half. I flashed to that moment in the forest, remembering how a musket had thrown a man into a tree, killing him before he hit the ground. I stood my ground, every muscle taut.

One man stepped forward, voice gruff.
"Stand down. We have orders to take this region by force."

I shook my head, tossing my pack aside.
"You'll have to go through me." My voice was louder than I felt. "None of you will leave here alive. Choose your battle wisely!"

I paced back and forth in front of them, provoking, making myself look bigger than I felt. I was outnumbered—but I wasn't alone. Behind me, townsfolk emerged: men and women with whatever they could grab—pitchforks, muskets, swords, even battered shields.

A silence settled, tense and brittle. Someone in the crowd behind me muttered,
"What are they waiting for?"
"A retreat," someone else whispered.
"*Quiet*!" another snapped.

I raised my sword high and slashed it down.
"*CHARGE!*"

With that, the tension snapped. Some enemies turned and fled, others stood and fought.
"*NONE OF THEM LEAVE THIS VALLEY ALIVE!*" I roared. As our makeshift army clashed with the invaders, the kingdom's gates slammed shut behind them. They were trapped.

From above, flames rose over the castle walls. Inside, mystics fought until the last but were overwhelmed. I spotted Rostov, striding up the steps to the castle, a wolf among sheep. My heart pounded—I bolted up the hill, dodging violence, and burst into the foyer. Verath's elegant decor lay smashed, trampled by boots.

Rostov was halfway up the elegant staircase, his face twisted in a cruel smile, a fresh claw mark running over his left eye. My hatred surged.

"*ROSTOV!*" I screamed. All the rage, all the loss, focused on him. He paused, savoring the moment, and then grinned wide.

"*Soon,* my sweet, I'll spill your blood and end our hunt. What a beautiful end we'll *share.*" His voice was mad, triumphant.

He whipped around, hair flying, and stalked up the stairs. I charged after him, just as he cornered a servant girl at the top. He raised his blade, but before he could strike, I pulled my flintlock and fired.

The shot punched through Rostov's hand. He dropped his sword, snarling, while the servant bolted. He laughed, a wild sound.

"YOU CANNOT STOP ME! I WILL ELIMINATE THE WEAK, AND SOON RHOVA WILL REMAIN STRONG!"

He turned and sprinted away, down the corridor. I drew my katana and chased him.

Rostov spun and attacked, his dagger flashing in three quick swipes. I ducked, swung for his stomach, slicing his fur shawl. He snarled, slashing wildly, nicking some of my hair. I rolled, clutching the strands, and he lunged again. This time, I ran, twisting through corridors, hearing him close behind.

I reached another staircase and hurried down, pulling out my flintlock. Rostov spotted me above and screamed,

"You can't run from me—I always catch my prey!"
He barreled down, but I shot him in the knee. He tumbled with a shriek.
"*YOU FUCKING BITCH!*" he howled.

Gunfire echoed behind me. I took the chance to bolt, cutting down two gunmen firing at someone behind a desk. The man I saved thanked me with a look of shock and ran. Blood on the floor caught my attention—a trail leading deeper under the steps.

I followed, nerves raw, trailing Rostov's blood through the winding corridors. Every step, I pictured what I'd do to him.

I burst into the throne room, saw another corridor veering off, and kept following the trail. Shouts rang out ahead, indistinct at first. When I drew closer, I saw Rostov yelling at Verath, who was standing cool and collected.

"Akira! *Welcome!*" Verath called, almost casual. Something about him was off, his demeanor too cheerful. Rostov turned, growling, then faced Verath again, blade raised despite his mangled hand.

"You are going to *die* today!" Rostov spat.

Verath just smiled and slipped behind a curtain. Rostov gave chase. I followed.

Beyond the curtain, sunlight spilled in through a great skylight. Dragons soared overhead, casting shifting shadows. Verath waited on a stage, a heavy curtain behind him. Rostov staggered, blood loss slowing him, but hate still burning in his eyes.

Verath pulled a cord. The curtain fell, revealing Drake—trapped in a glass tube. But he wasn't the same Drake I remembered. His hands pressed to the glass, glowing orange, eyes burning red. He saw me and, even in panic, tried to wave, shaking his head frantically. My mind flashed to the night Rostov had taken Drake by force, the orange eyes and defensive flames, what had Verath done to him?

Verath placed a hand on the glass.
"How could you not tell me you'd freed a *phoenix?* Akira, that's not something you keep secret." His eyes were full of awe—and calculation. "He has the power to fell entire kingdoms, and you have him wasting his skills on camping… My suspicions started as we were about to engage with the orcs in Ectwë when he shared some interesting information about a *last resort*? He also shared some other interesting information, *HE* killed Sara. So now I'm going to return the favor, I'm going to kill *him* and make you watch!" Verath was *Cavalier*, and *Furious.*

Rostov turned, stunned. "That changes nothing!"

But it did. Water began to fill the tube, rising past Drake's knees. Rostov, finally afraid, fled down a side corridor. Verath, already finished, strode off the stage.

My chest constricted. I ran up the steps, searching for anything to break the glass. I slammed my katana's hilt against it, screamed in frustration as cracks spiderwebbed but held. Water crept to Drake's waist.

Drake pressed his hand to the glass. His eyes met mine, and I felt my rage turn to terror—boiling tears streaming down my cheeks. I drew my flintlock—three shots left. He shook his head, but I fired once, and twice. The cracks deepened. I smashed the hilt into the glass, and it finally collapsed. Water gushed out, spilling Drake onto the stage.

Drake gasped for breath, then hugged me—tight, desperate. I let myself hold him for a heartbeat, then wriggled free. There was no time.

I tore down the stairs, chasing Rostov's blood trail.
"*Akira…!*" Drake's voice was hoarse.
I turned back, gave him a wry, preoccupied smile.
"What do you want, an *'I love you'*?"
He managed a crooked grin.
"Go. I'll be here." He said softly.

I pressed on, crashing through the final doors just as a gunshot rang out. Agony ripped through my leg—I hit the floor, cursing. Rostov had shot me, *again.* point-blank.

“Now we’re even.” He tossed the gun aside, limping, blood dripping down his leg.

I slid up against the wall, gritting my teeth against the pain. The bullet was lodged in my thigh. Rostov coughed, eyes bright with fever.

“What have you been through that makes you so damn near *invincible*?” He laughed, then choked on blood.

I hobbled to my feet, katana in hand, looming over him.

Rostov smiled, blood on his teeth.
“Beware of your boyfriend out there—*phoenixes* are dangerous. Most *powerful* mystics known. They’ll burn their enemies to ash and move on to the rest. Not just a last resort—he’ll scorch the earth if you make him.”

I’d heard the stories of ancient mystics called *Phoenixes*. I’d never seen one—until *Drake*, but Drake doesn't seem *malicious*.

Rostov coughed up blood and leaned back, surrendering to fate.
“It seems I misjudged our hunt. I was the *prey.*” He managed a hollow laugh.

I let him speak. He wasn't leaving here alive—whether I killed him or not. He met my eyes, and I tapped two fingers to my left eye. He smirked.

"That leopard—thing of yours has a worse temper than you, had the unfortunate experience of meeting the end of his claws outside." Rostov's breath grew ragged.

He let out a last sigh. "Take New Zodan. Lead my men—you'll do it right. But don't trust Verath. He's not a good man." His skin paled, his eyes sunk. He closed his eyes, nodded once. "Do it *right…*"

He exhaled, long and final. I stared at his corpse, then fired the remaining round in my revolver into him for good measure. The flintlock clattered aside. I limped back for Drake, who managed a shaky smile.

"Where's *Atlas*? Who knew I'd miss the little guy?" Drake said, voice thin.

I actually laughed, despite the pain.
"He's not as little as you think."

We walked together, slow and battered, through the halls of the ruined castle. When we finally reached the foyer, people had gathered—shell-shocked, desperate for answers. We kept walking, Atlas waited up ahead, roaring in blood-soaked victory. We walked up a dirt path toward the port, leaving the crowd behind. “Good boy, Atlas.” I said as I scratched behind his ears.

Even with Rostov gone, I knew—the hunt was over, but my fight was *far from finished.*

Chapter 20: Let the Music Drown the War

Act I: Like Joy Knew Where to Find Us

I couldn't remember the last time I heard music that didn't sound like a funeral dirge.

Here, in the thick of the Eîthorian dock district, it rose like heat off the stone streets—messy, rowdy, off-key. *Glorious*. Someone had dragged a battered fiddle onto a crate and was sawing through it like it owed them a debt. The crowd didn't care. They danced anyway.

Drake and I had barely made it three steps into the tavern before someone handed me two mugs.

He grinned like a devil caught in daylight. "That for me or are you trying to poison someone?"

"It's free," I said, sniffing it. "So *probably* both." I cautiously handed him a mug.

"Excellent. Let's toast to questionable decisions."

Still, I drank. He did too. The first sip made my throat burn and my eyes water. The second tasted like something real.

We passed through waves of laughter, shoulders bumping ours, strangers shouting half-songs in languages I barely knew. There was blood on some of their clothes, ash on others, and not even one of them seemed to care. They were alive. They had survived. We had survived. That was enough.

Drake tilted his head toward the dancers.
"Dance?" His smile threatened to vanquish any darkness I'd surround myself with.

I raised a brow. "I don't dance." I said with a sly smile.

"You say that like it's a fact," he said, raising an eyebrow, already offering his hand.

"It is." I said firmly.

"Then I guess I'm about to witness a miracle. Make way!" he bellowed toward the dance floor. "The lady's about to create art."

I rolled my eyes so hard I nearly saw the back of my skull, but I let him pull me anyway.

And we danced.

Badly. Loudly. With no form or restraint. A full spin nearly knocked someone's chair over. Drake almost tripped on his own feet but pressed on. I forgot how to breathe around the third song, and I didn't care.

At one point he yelled, "I think we invented a new style of combat!"
I shouted back, "You mean *flailing?!*"

"Exactly! Very niche. Very underground." I giggled.

And then—mid-laugh, arms tangled from some half-step spin—he kissed me.

It wasn't planned; it wasn't poetic. Just a burst of breath and warmth between us in the flickering tavern light. I blinked, stunned—and then I kissed him back. Not out of desperation or survival this time, but something simpler. Something soft.

When we broke apart, he looked breathless and *triumphant.*

"See?" he said. "Told you, you *could* dance."

Even Atlas stayed—curled in the corner near the fire, eyes half-lidded, as if watching over us was enough to keep him calm. His tail flicked once when someone got too close. No one tried twice.

The tavern door creaked open again. One of the kids ducked back inside, cheeks red from the cold night air. He held something small and wooden in both hands, like it was treasure.

"Found this near the docks!" he shouted over the music, waving it at his friend. "Look at it!"

The other kid squinted. "What is that?"

"A dog, I think," the first one said, grinning. "Kinda cool, right? I heard a guy yelling outside but found this as I followed the sounds."

He held it up to the firelight. The figurine was rough—half its tail missing, one ear worn to a nub. The snout was chipped, and dark streaks stained the grain like it had been dropped in mud or blood or both. It looked like it had been through a lot to get here.

Drake didn't notice. He was busy explaining something about "fishing with your heart" to a baffled soldier from Khofte.

I saw it, though.

Just for a moment. Just long enough to wonder where it had come from, and why it felt… *heavy.*

The kid stuffed it into his coat and darted toward the music again, laughing.

I didn't ask. Some relics didn't need stories. And not everything washed up from the wreckage was meant to be understood.

Still—I watched the door a second longer before I turned back to the *warmth.*

Act II: As If We Were Meant to Rest

We didn't plan to stay the night. But somehow, we ended up with a room upstairs.

Drake had talked the innkeeper into it—probably with charm and a handful of promises we couldn't keep. I didn't ask. He tossed me the key like it was something he'd won.

"It's ours until sunrise," he said. "Maybe longer, if the world forgets we're here."

The room was small. Sloped ceilings. A single bed with too many blankets. A window cracked just enough to let in the scent of salt and chimney smoke.

We shut the door behind us and let the laughter from the tavern fade into a hum.

I kicked off my boots. Drake unlaced his shirt and pulled it off. Atlas leapt onto the bed first, curled at the edge like he'd been destined to be there before us.

I sat beside him, suddenly petting his bristled fur.

Drake got into bed and leaned back against the wall; He looked at me like he was trying to come up with something to say.

“Do you ever think about what comes after?” he asked.

“After what?” I said, trying not to yawn.

“All of this. The fighting. The running. The weight we carry.” He seemed conflicted.

I hesitated. “I’ve never really thought about it, this is all I’ve ever known, but no, I don’t think about it.”

“Why not?” His hand grasped mine. “You may be used to it, but this isn’t a sustainable way to live, Akira.” His tone was worrisome, but I knew he meant well.

I sighed and ruffled his hair, “only because I end up saving you repeatedly.” I said with a smirk.

He laughed, soft. “Fair. But I think we might get through this, we’ll go back to Sylhalin and help the people gain a sense of normalcy after Rostov, that city has seen some things.” His eyes lit up thinking about helping the elves heal after the tyranny.

That made me smile. Not a big one. But real.

He scooted closer, his hand brushing mine.
“I’m glad you’re here. Still, you’ve softened a lot since I met you a few weeks ago.”

I leaned against him.

“You make it easier to be,” I said.

The room smelled like salt and old wood and something warm I couldn’t name. We didn’t speak much after that. Just curled beneath the blankets, Atlas pressed against my legs, Drake’s arm draped over my waist.

There wasn't firelight. Just the moon, spilling cold silver across the floorboards.

Still, it felt warm.

And for one night, one fragile thread of time, joy didn’t feel like a rebellion.

It felt like a promise.

“Do you think Sylhalin has chickens?” Drake asked. “I wasn’t there long but I didn’t see one chicken.” His tone was as firm as stone as my laugh filled the dark room. “I really like them, I hope they do.”

Chapter 21: I Wasn't Supposed to Be This

Act I: The Evening Gods Looked Away

The docks were wrong.

Too narrow. Too loud. Too alive.

I stumbled barefoot, dragging my coat behind me. stained with something that had once been red and noble.

My hand hurt from gripping my dog figurine so tight.

I glanced down at it, all broken and twisted, a mangled memory of a man I respected, a man who deserved better.

I threw the dog as far as I could hoping distance would hurt me less.

It didn't.

I screamed at a gull.
It screamed back.
I *lost*.

"You all saw it," I growled, spinning to no one. "You saw her take it from me. Everything. —*Everything.* And you *clapped.*"

A man bumped into me with a crate.
I threw the crate into the sea. The man followed it.

"*YOU WILL NOT BRUSH ME ASIDE!*" I shouted at the water.

People scattered. Doors slammed shut. A dog barked once and was never seen again. I passed a tavern, lilting music filled the surrounding air like a suffocating fog.

Then I saw *her*.

Or—someone *close*.

She was younger. Taller. The scarf was green, not red.

But her walk. Her face.
The way she turned to look at me like she might say *something*— end *Everything*.

"Don't!" I shrieked.

My voice cracked like glass dragged across metal.

"Don't you dare look at me like *her*."

The girl froze. "I—*I don't*—"

"I SAID *DON'T!*" I bellowed.

And I was on her.

The scream echoed as I slammed her into a wall of crates. Fishermen screamed. A sailor tried to pull me back—I threw him five feet without touching him.

The girl choked. She tried to beg.

I didn't listen.

My fists were red before her body stopped shaking. Her scarf lay across my boot.

I stood over her, chest heaving. Eyes wide.

And then—

I saw *him*.

Darion.

Blonde. Gentle. Mouth slightly open like he wanted to say something again.

"*You—*" I whispered.

I dropped to my knees and crawled toward the ghost.

"I didn't mean to. I swear. You were doubting me, you wouldn't shut up, I just wanted you to *listen—*"

Then I was over him, on the road before Sylhalin after that terrible night in Ectwë, before I lost Sylhalin to that scum, Rostov. My hands around Darion's neck urging for him to breathe his last breath, his eyes filled with panic. Choking sounds filled the clearing until his movements slowed to nothing, his existence fading to an obstacle in the road.

Darion's ghost knelt too and said nothing.

"I tried to stop. I did. You were looking at me like *she did*—like I was wrong. And *I—*"

I broke; tears streamed down my cheeks.

The sob that left me didn't sound *human*.

"I didn't mean to kill you." I wept.

I curled forward, blood on my hands, on my face, on the wood under me.

"Why are you still *here*?" I whispered. "Why won't you *leave*?" I demanded.

But Darion just *stared.*

Just like Sam had.

Just like she *had*. Just like the girl I'd never know the name of. And I wept, alone, surrounded by silence and salt and screams I could never take back.

Act II: What's Left of Me Hates Me Too

I woke to the sound of wind scraping across the cold stones.

My back ached. My mouth tasted like rust. There was blood on my knuckles and something sticky dried in my hair.

I didn't remember sleeping.

I didn't remember stopping.

I sat up slowly. The dock was cold beneath me. My coat clung to my arms like wet cloth. There were no voices nearby—just waves, ropes creaking, and the sound of something loose flapping in the breeze.

I looked around.

No crowd. No guards. No Sam. No Darion.
No girl with the wrong smile.

Just the sea.

And the quiet.

I stood, stumbling once, catching myself on a barrel.

Everything hurt.

I turned a corner—toward the alley beside the grain shed—and saw myself.

My reflection in a puddle.

Red-eyed. Pale. Hollow. Still.

And then it moved.

Not with me. Not a mirror.
It looked up faster. Smirked.

"You look like *shit,*" it said.

I blinked and stumbled back.

"You should be dead, you know. Would've been *cleaner.*"

The voice was *mine*. But more *smug. Cruel.*

"I didn't—" My voice cracked. "I didn't mean to—"

"No one cares," the reflection snapped. "She's still alive. That's all they'll remember."

I clenched my fists. "Who are *you*?"

"I'm what's left of *you* that's *useful.*"

The reflection sneered. “You sat in the street and screamed at ghosts. You murdered a girl because she looked at you wrong. Do you think that’s something *kings* do?”

“I’m not—” I looked away. “I didn’t want to be—”

“*YOU’RE PATHETIC.*”

The voice rang through my skull like a cracked bell.

“Get up. Clean yourself. Get to the castle. Find what power you still have and *USE IT.”*

“I don’t even know who’s still with me,” I whispered. “I don’t know what’s *real—*”

“You don’t need real. You need a *PLAN*.”

The reflection leaned in, face twitching with disgust.

“Or do you want to die here? Stained. Stupid. Forgotten?”

I reached toward the water.

“I have *questions—”*

But the reflection was gone.

Just water now. Just my face. Blank. Trembling.

"WAIT!" I screamed.

Silence.

"COME BACK!" I begged.

I grabbed a crate and hurled it at the puddle. Wood splintered. Water sprayed.

Then I began tearing through barrels. Kicking walls. Smashing glass. Screaming not at the people—but at the absence.

"COME BACK! ANSWER ME! I DIDN'T MEAN TO BE THIS!"

I dropped to my knees.

Breathing heavy.

Alone again.

Always alone.

Chapter 22: Not Yet, But Close

Act I: Just Close Enough

She stole *my* blanket.

I woke up cold and confused, the fire little more than coals, sunlight filtered in the small window of our room and Akira curled up on the other side of it—wrapped like a smug cocoon in what had very clearly been *my blanket.*

She'd even tucked it under her arms. That was the part that got me.

I sat up slowly, joints protesting, breath puffing white in the early morning air.

She didn't move.
Didn't stir.

But I saw it—
The corner of her mouth twitched like she was trying not to laugh.

So, she *was* awake.

"*Really?*" I said, voice low.

No answer.

I crawled around the fire and knelt beside her.

"*Akira.*" I chirped.

Still nothing.

I leaned down, closer. "You know I'm going to steal it back."

Her eyes opened—*barely*—and she whispered, *"Try it."*

I didn't.

Because I was warm already.
Just seeing her there—content, teasing, safe—*was enough*.

I settled beside her, using my arm as a pillow, close but not touching.

She turned her face toward me and gave me a sleepy smile.

"You talk in your sleep," I said.

"I *don't* sleep." She stated, her eyes clearly closed.

"You *do.*" I pushed coyly.

"I don't *talk* either." She snapped.

“You said my name.” I teased.

She didn’t respond.

She smiled—barely—and closed her eyes again.

And I thought—
If this is all I ever get, it’s *enough*.

Act II: Down, and Still Falling

I trained each morning.
Before the fire burned down. Before she woke.

I walked along the docks until I found a small beach to train on.

The waves helped me think.

Feel.

It wasn't a habit—it was survival, she taught me that.
My muscles ached if I didn't use them. My thoughts were worse.

This morning, I spun the staff low—swept the sand, turned, struck upward toward nothing.
Again.

And *again*.

Controlled.

Fluid.

Repeat until the silence *stopped* screaming.

I didn't hear her come up behind me.
But I felt her.

She let me finish the sequence.
Then stepped forward—
And took the staff from my hands.

No warning. No explanation.

She twirled it once—*awkwardly*—and raised a brow.

"You're going too easy on yourself," she said with a slight smile.

I blinked. "It's not for fighting, it helps me think."

"No?" she asked. "Then why does it move like a weapon?"

I didn't answer. She was always so survival oriented. She didn't opt for nonessential things; she preferred the bare minimum to get through the day alive.

She gripped it like she'd done it before—lower stance, a playful edge in her posture.

"Come on," she said.

"I'm not going to spar with you." I stated.

She lunged.

I dodged.

She grinned and gave a giggle.

And that was how it started.

The duel was nothing and everything.
She was fast. Not stronger, not heavier, but faster.
She moved like she had wind in her lungs and fire in her legs.

Her hair swayed as fast as her strikes.

And when she swept my feet out from under me, she didn't even gloat.

She just stood there,
Staff braced against the ground,
Hand outstretched.

"You'll get there," she said, smiling.

And that broke something in me.

Not because she knocked me down.
But because she didn't look surprised.
Like she already knew what I was made of.

I took her hand.

And I thought—I want more of *this*.
More of her mornings. Her breath. Her fire.

Not just today.
Not just until we return to Sylhalin.
Always.

Chapter 23: What We Almost Said

Act I: This Was Almost Peace

We made camp at the edge of Eîthor's valley, just before the long stretch toward Sylhalin.
The ruins were behind us now. The hunt was over. And for the first time in weeks, Akira let herself stop moving.

She braided her hair when she was nervous. I'd learned that much.

She did it fast—too *fast*—and then undid it, fingers working again. Like the tension had nowhere else to go.

We hadn't spoken much today. There wasn't anything to say. The world was holding its breath.

I sat near the fire pit, stirring through the half-dead coals. They hissed but didn't catch. The kind of warmth that pretended to be more than it was.

"You want me to scout ahead?" I asked.

She didn't turn. "You'd get lost."

"Probably." I laughed, my soul hurt after what I did to that poor girl, *Sara*, but I did it for her…

She went back to braiding. Slower, this time.

I stood, crossed to her. My legs ached. I ignored it.

She didn't look up when I crouched beside her. Just kept weaving. Focused like it mattered. Maybe it did.

I reached for the braid.

She stilled—just for a second—but didn't stop me.

"I won't mess it up," I said. "*Maybe…*"

The strands felt smoother than I expected. I didn't know if I'd ever braided anyone's hair before, but my hands remembered something. I worked in silence. Careful. Gentle. I didn't want to give her a reason to pull away.

When I finished, she reached back and touched it.

Like she didn't quite believe it was real.

I sat beside her in the grass. The sun was lower now—turning gold over the ridge.

"You ever thought about not going back?" I asked.

She didn't say anything.

"Sylhalin. Orders. All of it, just because Rostov left it to you, doesn't mean you have to."

She shrugged. "That's what I have to do."

"Doesn't have to be."

She looked at me. "If I don't, someone worse than Rostov can take his place, I *have* to."

And gods—I didn't say it. I didn't have to.

But if she'd asked me to stay with her, for everything to come.

Right then, right *there*—

I would've agreed.

Act II: Sketched in Firelight

She was sketching.

The paper was creased, half-torn, smudged with mud at the corners, but she held it like it meant something. Knees pulled up, back resting against her pack. Head bowed.

I didn't know what she was drawing.

I didn't ask, I'd learned to keep most questions to myself around her, if she wanted to tell me, she would on her own.

The fire was burning low. Atlas was asleep, tail twitching. The wind had died sometime in the last hour, and the night was holding still around us.

I kept reading the way she moved—eyes flicking down, then up again, then down. The way she chewed the inside of her cheek when she concentrated. The way her fingers kept adjusting the grip like she was trying to make the charcoal say something she couldn't.

I'd never seen her this quiet while awake.

"You don't show people that," I said.

She looked up. Blinked. "What?" She asked, confused.

"The drawing. You *always* hide it when I'm around."

She looked down at the paper, then back at me.

"It's not done." She stated.

"Let me see it anyway."

She hesitated. But she didn't say no.

She turned it around slowly. Not dramatic—just careful. Like it might fall apart between her hands.

It was… a landscape. Hills. Trees. Our camp. And two figures near the fire.

One of them was unmistakably *me.*

"You made me taller," I said.

"You sit like *you're* taller," she said with a smile.

I looked at the sketch again. At how detailed it was. At how gently she'd drawn the shadows around my shoulders.

"You see me like that?" I asked bewildered.

She didn't answer right away.

"I don't know how else to see you."

I didn't know what to say to that.

So, I just handed the paper back.

She tucked it away like it had never existed.
Like that moment didn't shift the ground under us.

But it did.

And later, lying under the stars, not sleeping, not even pretending to, I let myself think—

Maybe she already knows.
And maybe I don't need to say it.

Part III: There Was No Mercy in the End

Chapter 24: Back to step one

I stood on the balcony of my castle, watching the group in the courtyard slowly repair the damage from the raid. My head rang on a loop. My clothes were tattered; my hair crusted with blood that used to be on my hands. My face was black and blue from various injuries, and I struggled to follow my reflection's instructions from the day before. Who was he? My *conscience*?

Laurel walked in during my deep contemplation.

"Sir? The castle is a mess. Rostov's corpse is in the dining room. There's water and broken glass throughout the ballroom," she said, clearly surprised.

I turned and gave her a wary smile. "Ready the troops for the reclamation of Sylhalin."

She nodded shakily, "sir, I just wanted to extend my condolences for Sam, I know you two were close friends, also I have heard concerns about one of our own's disappearance, 'Darion' no one has seen him since you returned, do you happen to—" "WHY IS EVERYONE SO OBSESSED WITH THIS ONE MAN'S DISAPPERANCE?!" I screamed in fury, cutting her off mid-sentence and throwing a vase from the bedside table. She quickly fled the room. I followed slowly behind. I thought of Sam and quickly pushed it from my mind. Things were in my favor—even if they weren't going according to plan.

I entered the courtyard and was greeted by the skeleton force of my troops. The rest had been killed or injured the night before. I ordered Laurel to recruit from the dockside town nearby and bring in new soldiers for training. She eyed me closely before she headed down the path as the rest of my followers and I turned toward Sylhalin.

The air still held the weight of death, even though the corpse piles had vanished. The ground bore scorched marks, which had faded with time.

As we approached the gate, we waited for it to rise.

It *didn't*.

"HEY! RAISE THE GATE!" I shouted. The gatekeepers looked worried and disappeared behind the wall.

Then Akira approached the inner gate, her scowl oozing confidence and authority.

"You are not welcome. *Leave*," she said, her tone rising.

I took a deep breath and slammed my fist into the new slatted metal gate. "You don't understand what you're starting. THIS CITY IS MINE!"

People ran past behind her—some laughing, others singing. Life was returning to normal in Sylhalin.

I glared at her for a long moment. Then her cub jumped from the top of the wall, landing behind her with a growl. It seemed she had the blacksmith make him armor. Atlas now wore fitted plating across his body, making him a much bigger threat.

I turned and headed down the hill, ordering my people to follow.

The gate burst to life and began to rise.

"Come with me. You touch *nothing,*" Akira snapped. Her voice stopped my followers cold. She was addressing *me*.

"Let's go," she said, rolling her eyes as she turned toward the center of town.

So much for *not* being welcome.

I kept up with her, but her guards stepped in front of my followers. They were not permitted to enter.

I caught up until we were walking side by side. "This city is *mine*. Rostov is *dead*. It returns to *me*." I explained sternly.

Akira turned, unamused. "Rostov ordered me to take the city. *I* was with him when he took his last breath. *I* pursued him, backed him into a corner. *I* control the city. *You* are *not* welcome. Are we *clear*?" She turned and placed her hands on her hips, her armor was upgraded, more regal, but efficient, it makes me *sick*.

She had a confidence I hadn't heard from her before—like she already knew she was *superior.*

I stepped closer. "You're making a mistake. You'll see it *soon enough.*" I seethed.

I was about to grab her arm—but her aggressive cub forced me to step back.

"Escort this man to the southern gate. Make sure he *doesn't* return."

Two soldiers grabbed me by the arms and dragged me away. They tossed me through the gate and lowered it.

I must've blacked out, because all I remember after all that screaming until nothing, but darkness surrounded me.

—

Until I woke up in my bedroom.

I sat up and rang the service bell. A man appeared shortly after.

“Sir?”

I ran a hand through my hair and requested a cup of coffee. I was up. Might as well stay up.

The man nodded and left.

I was still *furious*. Akira had the gall to take my city—*mine*.

I stood and approached the floor-length mirror. I wore silk pajamas I didn’t remember changing into. I stared into my reflection.

“*You can’t let her live. You know that. She’ll only be a bigger thorn in our side. KILL HER. KILL HER! DO IT!*”

I shook my head furiously, and my reflection returned to normal.

I turned and walked out to the balcony. The sun was beginning to set.

The northern gate rattled open.

A wagon rolled down the path toward my castle.

I'll admit—I was intrigued. Access to the valley is extremely limited. Whoever this was, they had serious connections. Especially with Akira trying to keep me out of Sylhalin.

I approached the gate. The woman driving looked familiar—her posture, the way she carried herself. It was Priya. She wore tattered clothes—a grey button-up and brown denim pants. Odd, considering the last time I saw her, she wore a red floor length ballgown.

I waved off the guards and approached with a polite smile.

"What brings you to Eîthor? I already met with Cilmair. We haven't forged a deal just yet." I said, examining her wagon.

Priya shook her head. "This visit is unrelated. Cilmair requests your presence in Lolem for the Lunar Eclipse Festival in a day. She plans to use the festivities to introduce your new position of power. She believes the citizens will be too preoccupied to revolt."

She had a point. Premature—but smart.

I turned toward the castle gate, but Priya stopped me.

"Where are you going? You need to come with me now."

I gave her a confused look. “You said by tomorrow. Why must we leave now?”

She sighed. “Sylhalin’s security has been reworked. No one knows why. But there are travel restrictions. It’s best to get you to Lolem before they tighten some more.”

I wanted to protest—but I knew she was right.

Soon, I was climbing into the back of her wagon, hoping we’d get through unscathed.

We passed the first gate without trouble. I peered through a slit in the fabric.

The city looked normal again—maybe even better. People smiled, despite their injuries.

After a while, Priya coughed—*a signal.*

The wagon suddenly lurched forward. The horses began stomping in panic. Screams rang out. Then we were flying.

“Are we at the gate?” I yelled.

Priya laughed—an unnerving, thrilled sound. The gate rose just enough to let us through. Guards shouted. More wagons followed behind us.

Gunfire erupted.

I stumbled toward the front. "CAN'T YOU DRIVE STRAIGHT?!"

She grinned back at me, laughing again.

We tore through Calís, what once was a peaceful countryside between Sylhalin and Lolem was now being smashed through everything from gazebos to tents. The soldiers behind us shouted, shots firing past.

Priya sped toward the Lolem gate, which began to rise.

I ducked low, trying not to get shot.

"WHY ARE THEY CHASING US? WHAT DID YOU DO?!"

Priya didn't answer. Just smiled—wild and knowing—and kept driving.

We crossed the Lolem threshold. The gate dropped behind us with a thud, crushing one of the wagons. Guards detained two of the pursuers.

Priya sighed in relief.

I stared, stunned, as we rolled into the most beautiful city I'd seen in years.

Tall buildings. Lights. Waterfalls. Cilmair's palace rose at the city's peak, glowing with magic and power. Aqueducts fed fountains. A lake swirled below.

Priya approached. "Astounding, right? Cilmair isn't great personally, but professionally? She's unmatched."

We walked uphill together.

"Cilmair built a haven for engineers and scientists—freethinkers who'd have perished without her. They owe her everything."

Her pride was obvious.

The people here didn't seem oppressed like other Light Kingdoms.

We reached a marble staircase. At the top was a courtyard with a massive fountain. Children ran between tables and lanterns for the festival.

We continued upward.

Silence fell between us, but Priya's energy remained bright.

The final staircase was the largest.

As we climbed, I felt a tingle climb my spine.

A line of the dead stood along each step.

Watching me.

Most were unfamiliar—but not all.

At the top stood Sam.

My friend. My closest.

Guilt crushed my lungs.

He wouldn't have died if I hadn't brought him with me to Ectwë.

The souls stared—but then they began to clap.

Silent, but clear.

Why?

Priya walked through Sam and turned back.

"I'll take you to your chambers and inform the queen."

We stepped through the palace gate and waited at a moat. The drawbridge dropped with a crash.

“Why so many precautions?” I asked. “Cilmair’s powerful—but no one would go this far to kill her.”

Priya shrugged and led me inside.

The foyer looked like an overgrown forest; ivy draped over stone. A grand staircase split in two.

She led me upstairs, past carved doors and flowering vines, and opened one to the right.

My room.

A bed. A desk. A closet. A private bath.

Perfect.

I thanked her. She smiled and left.

I collapsed onto the bed, clothes and all—and fell into a deep sleep.

I woke to the frantic ringing of a bell.

A man in ragged clothes stood above me.

“You’re requested in the dining room, sir.”

I sat up and followed the smell of food, stumbling upon Cilmair and Priya seated alone.

I sat down. The servants—all dressed in rags—filled my plate and vanished.

I stared at the food.

Cilmair spoke without looking up. “Don’t waste it. Wartime’s hard enough. Malnutrition helps no one.”

I began to eat. The food smelled better than it looked.

We ate in silence.

When she finished, Cilmair set down her fork.

“Verath,” she said. “You are *not* a well-liked man. To give you full control would be *reckless*. But *if* I introduce you during the Eclipse Festival—*if* I give you a small taste of power while the people celebrate—they won’t revolt. I’ll call you out on the balcony after my speech. Then you do… *whatever* it is you *do.*” She said dismissively.

She was confident.

I nodded. I didn’t have a choice.

Lolem's engineers would advance my plans more than Sylhalin ever could. And with Rostov gone, Zodan was open. After Sarnawen, only Kishak remained. Khofte wouldn't fight—they were too weak.

But *Camilla?*

The queen without a face.

The royal without a vendetta?

Time to change that.

Chapter 25: When the Moon Rose Just for Us

Act I: Until the Moon Rises

I stood in the glass room of the observatory of Sylhalin when Drake approached from behind me with a glass of wine in each hand. I gave a mellow smile and turned back to the view of the city. Of all the sights of Rhova, I could see the highest peaks of Khofte where the dragons swarmed, the valley of Eîthor, the blessed walls of Rhín, and the elven city of Sylhalin below.

"It's quite the view," Drake said as he took a deep breath.
I took a sip of wine. "Yes, it is."
I gave a light chuckle. For the first time, I felt content.
"Cheers," Drake said with a smile.
"Cheers."
We clinked our glasses and each took a sip.

Our quiet moment was interrupted by a frantic soldier who had climbed the stairs and stopped to catch his breath.
"Ma'am, a wagon has breached the eastern gate."
He leaned down, hands on his knees to remain on his feet.
I approached the east-facing window. Sure enough, the gate was raised, and a convoy of horse-drawn wagons rampaged through the village of Calís.

I let out a sigh. "Well, they're being pursued, so I don't see a reason to worry much about it. Close the gate—and it remains closed until I say so."
The soldier nodded, gave a bow, and disappeared down the stairs.

I sighed and turned my attention back to Drake. "Where were we?"
In response, he finished his wine and took my hand. "Come with me."
He seemed eager, almost excited, to lead me toward something. I gave him a confused smile and followed.

We descended into the foyer of the observatory and found Atlas sleeping in his armor. Atlas stirred at our departure, "No, you stay buddy, we'll be back." I said softly. Atlas took my dismissal and went to sleep. Drake pulled me through the door and toward the stables.
"Where are we going?" I asked with a chuckle.
"No questions—just experience."
I rolled my eyes at his vague response.

We mounted two horses and rode off toward the northern countryside of Sylhalin. We passed farms with cows, pigs, and vegetables. I kept close to Drake, who seemed to know where he was going.

As we rode, the ocean began to close in on our left, and the eastern wall of the kingdom loomed on the right. Drake slowed down and hopped off his horse. There was a small cottage nearby, but ahead of us was the ocean—all the way to the horizon—and on that horizon sat icebergs. The sun was beginning to set, and the moon was starting to rise. The sky behind the icebergs took on a gorgeous blue hue, with specks of white invading the space. Even without the moon in full view, the clash of day and night brought bright orange against the deepest blues, merging together in the distance.

I let out a gasp. *Breathtaking.*

Drake walked over to his saddlebags and pulled out a blanket. He laid it on the ground and then untied a basket from his horse. He set up glasses, plates, and candles on the blanket. I gave him a small smile and sat down as he motioned for me to.

"I apologize if this seems odd. We haven't known each other for more than a month and a half, but I felt this would be a good, quiet time to get to know each other even better," he said.

I raised a finger to his lips.

"It's alright. It's *perfect*," I reassured him.

He gleamed with excitement. I turned back toward the icebergs as he poured us some more wine.

Drake smiled and passed me a glass. I gasped again—penguins were sliding down the icebergs and splashing into the water in small groups.

"Do you mind if I ask you some questions?" he asked, the question made my mind fly to our second night together, but now his smile was light and genuine, like he was happy just to be here.
I gave a nod and prepared myself.

"What was your life like before meeting me?" he asked.
I considered his words.
"*Lonely*. It was lonely. I lived on my own for a couple of years. Never stayed somewhere for long—it was a very nomadic life. I kept to myself a lot."
I paused, then added, "Do I get to ask a question now?"
I had never told anyone much about me—not even Count Dendrin.

Drake nodded.

I pulled out the leather-bound diary from my pack.
"Did you know the woman who wrote this? *Theresa*?"
His face took on a saddened grin. He took a deep breath.
"Yes, I did."
I looked down at the diary in my hands, tracing the ragged leather's texture.
"She was my *wife*." He said softly.

I looked up in surprise.
"*Wife?*"
I tried to sound calm, but it completely lost me. I flipped through the pages.
Theresa didn't say they were married. No mention of that.

My heart went cold.
"*Mixa…?*"
Drake nodded, got up and pulled a small teddy bear out of his saddlebag.
"Mixa was my daughter. Theresa and I, we were married for six years."
He replied. My heart *sank*.

I opened my mouth, but nothing came out. He tried to hold back tears, but they began to drench the bear.

Drake took a deep breath and gave me a forced smile.
"I may have lost them, but I won't forget them. And that's what matters, I live my life as they would, and that's enough I think, Mixa didn't like hurting people, so since then I try to avoid killing." His voice broke.

He looked at me with tear-soaked eyes.
"What was your life like before you started living on your own? You showed me your village. May I ask what happened to it?" He said in between sniffles.

I looked toward the horizon. The penguins were still sliding down the icebergs.
"It was good. I lived with my mom, but…"
I planted my face in my hands. I took a moment, then continued.

"…My father died when I was an infant, and my mother was murdered when I was thirteen."
My face grew hot. I blinked back tears.

"A man threw me into a wagon with a cage filled with other kids from my village. He killed my mother when she tried to reach me. I can still see his face. Every detail."
My voice broke.

"She ran for me, fighting with all she had, when he jammed a sword through her head. It emerged through her forehead, holding her on her feet—but she was gone. Her eyes went dark. Her jaw fell. And he pushed her off with his foot."

Drake's eyes grew wide—*utterly* shocked.

I hid my face in my hands and began to sob. When I looked up, I choked back another sob.
"When I *first* left to be on my own, I was hunting the man who *killed* my mother. I was going to make him *regret* it—make him watch me kill *everyone* he loved while he watched from a cage."

My tears blurred my vision. I couldn't even see Drake anymore.

I took a deep breath.
"But my mother wouldn't agree with vengeance. She would say: 'Akira, forgiveness is the strongest weapon

you can yield. Anger only makes you feel worse in the end.'"

And she would've been right.

Drake set a sympathetic hand on my shoulder.
"I'm… *so*… sorry."

He began blowing out the candles and packing things away. I wiped my face.
"What are you doing?" I asked.

"I feel like this was poorly planned. I wanted this to be joyful, memorable. But now I see it was a mistake." he said urgently.

I reached for his hand.
"This went as good as it could have," I said with a weak smile.

He paused, as if considering something.

Then Drake reached into the basket and pulled out a small, uniquely carved box.
He opened it and smiled.
"Akira, will you be my wife?"

His words echoed in my head.

I tried to speak, but couldn't, I was stunned.

Drake continued.
"This was my late wife's ring. She gave it to me before the elders began the ritual to protect our village. She told me to give it to the next woman to take my heart and my hand. It was her final plea."

I stood and began to pace.
"Why are you asking? This seems sudden, we've only known each other a month and a half…"

Drake smiled.
"You are the strongest person I've ever met—in this age or the last. You inspire me to be better. You carry a weight that makes everyone around you want to fight harder. You are a *force* of nature, Akira. You make me brave. *You*, my dear, are *legendary.* And I would be lucky if you would agree to be my wife."

His words left me *oddly* flattered.

I rolled my eyes and sat back on the blanket.
He raised his glass.
"Let's toast to the pain. To the bad days. To opting for the better. I just want to be happy—and you, Akira, you make me happy. So, let's toast to the tears of our past, and the euphoria of our future."

He gave me a big, goofy smile.

I let out a sigh and rolled my eyes, then raised my glass. I tried to hide it, but I shared the same feelings.
"Cheers," I said, returning the smile.

We clinked glasses and sat there, watching the penguins in the distance. Drake wrapped his arm around me—and I felt a feeling I thought had died a long time ago.

Joyful.

Cheers indeed.

Act II: When the Stars Stopped Singing

I laid there, listening to Drake's mellow breathing, staring at the flames in the fireplace. Drake rolled over and greeted me.

"Good morning. How'd you sleep?" he asked, trying—*unsuccessfully*—to hide the tiredness in his voice.

"I slept fine. First time I've slept in a nice bed in a long time," I replied, distracted as I turned the ring on my finger. A golden band, encrusted with tiny diamonds—it was beautiful, extravagant, the most lavish thing I've ever owned.

Drake sat up and kissed my cheek.
"The perfect way to celebrate our wedding is the Lunar Eclipse Festival in Lolem. No killing, no life-or-death choices. Just an elegant night of food and all the liquor you can drink."

I groaned.
"I don't think it's a good idea. Lolem has some of the highest security in Rhova. I doubt we'll even get in. And I've been away from Atlas too long as of late."

I stood and began dressing, strapping on my sword and grabbing my pack. Drake scrambled up, hopping around trying to get one pant leg on. I tossed him the rest of his clothes and stepped outside, loading my pack into the saddlebag.

Drake followed, still struggling with his clothes. I mounted my horse and rode ahead at a slow pace to give him time. The roads back to the city were quiet, and I let the silence settle.

When we arrived, I led my horse into his stall. Drake caught up.

"I still think we should go. It's tonight, and all the other rulers will be there—it just makes sense," he said, trailing off like he *wanted* permission.

"The festival's for the rich, the sophisticated. Probably a dress code. Neither of us has anything elegant enough," I said, rolling my eyes as I left the stables. But Drake tugged my arm and led me toward the marketplace.

"We'll get something fashionable enough to get us through the door." He pleaded.

We passed stalls until we reached a seamstress. She was working a loom but stood the moment we arrived. She towered over me and extended a hand with dramatic flair.

"*Francesca*. How can I help you?"

Drake's peasant grin froze on his face. He hesitated, swallowed, then explained our need for festival attire.

Francesca gave a small smile, grabbed my hand, and led me into her tent. She opened a large trunk and began sifting through it.
"The Lunar Eclipse Festival is *exclusive*," she said. "You two don't seem like the *royal* type."

I smiled patiently.
"My *husband* insisted. I don't agree, but we hold this kingdom. So, it's not as if we *don't* meet the requirements." I stated confidently, almost defensively.

I sat near the exit, watching her work. I could've sworn she had a five o'clock shadow.

After a few minutes, Francesca gasped and lifted a dress—a deep midnight blue that faded to lighter blue, then purple. She thrust it at me.

"You must try it." She said sternly.

I took the dress, and she turned to the exit and vanished. I examined it, then stripped off my armor and tried it on. I called for her.

She returned, gasped again, and nodded in approval. "*Stunning*. Now for the rest."

She handed me blue heels and a translucent shawl. I slipped them on and stood before a floor-length mirror. Francesca approached, swept my hair into a bun, and gave a satisfied smile.

"*Breath-taking*."

She exited and ushered Drake inside, then promptly shooed me out. People on the street gawked. I tried to re-enter to get my clothes, but she threw shoes at me *every time*. I sighed and sat in front of the loom, chin in hand, *waiting*.

Eventually, Drake emerged in a tuxedo with a black tie. He spun for me with pride. I laughed—he looked *ridiculous*, but *endearing*.

Drake tried to hand Francesca a bag of gold. She refused. "Consider them a gift for your nuptials. Congratulations, I *do* love seeing two people in love."

She gave me back my armor, and I changed inside the tent. I bagged the dress and shoes, grabbed my scarf, and stepped out. Drake followed, and we walked slowly through the streets.

"You were beautiful back there," he said, smiling from ear to ear.

I patted his arm and rolled my eyes.

"I *know...*" I gave a dreamy sigh, "when am I not?" Drake gave me the biggest laugh; we had to stop walking so he could catch his breath again.

A convoy of wagons tore through the intersection, nearly running us over. Drake shouted and waved his fist.

We returned to the observatory. Atlas greeted me, standing and resting his legs on my shoulders. He was growing fast.

Later that evening, I stood watching Lolem light up—lanterns rising into the night sky, a shifting aura glowing over the city. Drake climbed the stairs in his tuxedo.

"You're not dressed?" he asked.

I turned and rested a hand on his shoulder.
"I have a *bad* feeling about this. I *can't* explain it, but my gut says *stay away from that festival.*"

Drake laughed and kissed my hand.
"I wouldn't let anything happen to you. I promise."
"Are you *kidding*? Out of the *two* of us? I won't let *anything* happen to *you.*" he gave me a chuckle, "Get dressed please." His words extracted a sigh from me, I reluctantly obliged.
I watched him descend the stairs before I changed into the dress, wrapped the shawl around me, tied up my hair. No matter what I did, two strands still fell over my face. I

looked out the window once more, then made my way downstairs—*carefully*, so I didn't die in these shoes.

At the top of the foyer steps, I spotted Drake. I descended. He watched me closely, stunned.

"*Wha…?*" he breathed.

I smiled nervously; I felt so vulnerable without my chainmail. He opened the door and bowed. A horse-drawn carriage waited. He ran ahead, opened it, and I climbed in. The carriage rattled to life.

Atlas sat there for a moment, watching us go, before staff led him inside. I exhaled and folded my hands in my lap. Anxiety twisted my insides into knots like it was trying to wring them dry.

We reached the city gate. It rose as we approached. At the palace, we exited the carriage, arms interlocked. Townspeople whispered as we passed—but to my knowledge, none of it was negative.

We ascended the final staircase. A moat surrounded the palace, and we entered via drawbridge. Inside, a crowd moved down a hall toward a ballroom. We followed.

The ballroom held a stage with five chairs—likely for the royals. Servants circled with trays of food and drink. Guests mingled.

Drake and I went to the bar. He ordered us mulled wine. We drank and observed the chaos around us.

A woman took the stage and addressed the room, though I couldn't make out her words. Then musicians appeared and launched into energetic music. Couples paired off and danced gracefully.

"Dance with me?" Drake asked, extending a hand.

I declined and took a sip of wine. He shrugged, walked backward into the crowd.

"Your loss." He said with a confident smile. "Someone here will enjoy my loving touch."

He disappeared. A man tapped my shoulder.

"What's a beautiful woman like you doing sitting alone at a party?"
He was old. Spit clung to his words. *Repulsed*, I tried to remain polite.

He set his drink down and traced the scar on my left cheek.
"How did you come by such a brutal mark?"

He bit his lip when he touched my face. I grabbed his wrist, slammed it into the bar, spilling his drink. "Touch me again, and I'll do much worse than a bruise." I whispered in his ear. He growled and slapped me.

"You stupid wench!" he yelled.

Blood ran from the reopened cut on my cheek. I kneed him in the groin. He collapsed to the floor. I grabbed my drink and walked off, searching for Drake.

I tried to keep to the wall but couldn't find him. Near the stage, I spotted *Verath*—laughing with a group. His eyes met mine. His smile stayed, but his eyes went *hollow*. He wasn't pleased to see me, *what* was he doing here? I caught myself wondering.

"Hey! —there you are. I couldn't find you at the bar," Drake said, reappearing.
"I was looking for you too!" I said, matching his relief.

The musicians began a slow song. Couples joined hands.

"Last chance," Drake said with a sly smile.

I rolled my eyes and nodded. We danced.

As we moved, I observed the crowd. They all seemed joyful, celebrating the eclipse and harvest. I didn't see the connection, but I wasn't about to ruin anyone's fun.

Drake tried to meet my eyes.

"*Where* are you?" He asked in a concerned tone.

"I'm *right* here," I replied, fixing my smile.

He didn't believe me.
"No, you're not. So *where* are you?" His smile had vanished leaving only worry.

I scanned the room for Verath. But he was gone.

"Fine," Drake muttered in irritation.

We danced in silence.

Fireworks cracked outside. The song ended. Drake turned and walked away.

"*Drake…!*" I called.

He was gone. I searched the hallway—*nothing.*

Then something caught my eye through the window. A beam of light?

It grew larger. It passed the city wall. It wasn't light—it was a dragon, flames pouring from its mouth. Houses ignited. Screams rose.

Then explosions. Flaming projectiles struck the castle. Four more dragons followed the first. My brain snapped back to the tavern in Eîthor, *"Sarnawen may just take out Lolem too just for allying with Verath."* The hair on the back of my neck, how could I have been so blind. "*EVERYBODY OUT NOW!!*" I ordered motioning people out.

Panic erupted. Guests fled the ballroom.

One fireball soared straight for the window.

I gasped, trying to jump out of the way.

Too late.

The explosion sent me flying. I crashed into a wall. Drapes and carpet caught fire. I tried to sit up—but collapsed. The world went black.

Chapter 26: Greatness Beneath the Deep

Act I: Elegy for the Moonlit City

"*Ow…*" I gripped my head and sat up. I attempted to stand but collapsed from dizziness. There were screams coming from the ballroom. A giant flaming boulder had collapsed the corridor and the doorway to it. I slowly crawled to the wall and used it to stand, taking my time to prevent the dizziness. I reached for my forehead and a staggering pain spread from the throbbing wound—no blood, but certainly a bruise. I looked out the towering window next to me. The dragons and fireballs were still flying over the whole city wreaking havoc and seemed to be aiming for the dam behind the palace.

They're trying to flood the city.

My spine began to shudder.

Drake.

I proceeded down the hallway and entered the crumbling foyer.

"DRAKE?!"

Guests were running down the steps and out the door. I ran across the drawbridge. It began to rise before I had reached the end, and I fell into the shallow moat below. I swam up to the ledge and climbed out. I caught my breath and ran down the stairs. A group of archers had tasked themselves with taking down the dragons above but weren't making much progress. I continued down the steps and was met with the remainder of the crowd in the courtyard; those left were either dead or wailing in grief over their loved ones. I ran past the group, preoccupied with my own mission and proceeded down the next staircase.

I had finally reached the city street, but just as I did, one of the fireballs slammed into the dam at the left side of the palace. It began to crack and crumble. A giant wave crashed down into the courtyard. I ran into the nearest house and slammed the door. The water flooded the streets. People screamed as they were swept away with the fury of the waves. I held the door shut, but water began to flood down the staircase across the room. It started rising faster than my mind could keep up with. I kept my head above the water until I couldn't anymore, forced to hold my breath or die here, I'd never find Drake, I'd never see Atlas again, I'd never get out of this waterlogged tomb of a city.

I swam up the steps and into a bedroom. I found a window. I rammed myself into it full force, but it refused to shatter. I removed my heel and slammed it into the window like a blade. *Once. Twice.* And then a third time—the window buckled beneath the weight of my desperation. The glass began to sink into the unknown in slow motion. I swam through the gap, chopping through the surrounding tragedy and upwards towards the surface. My head burst up from the depths, and I was met with the screams and chaos I had left. But those left were on the rooftops of the taller buildings of the city. I swam to the nearest building and collapsed onto the solid ground. I lay there breathless, staring at the colorful lanterns floating to the sky, this celebration, now forever clung to the name: *Horror.*

Tonight, had taken a terrible turn.

I shakily sat up and looked towards the marble palace, its peak still competing with the sky—or what was left of it.

My stomach sank. The tallest floors were in the towers toward the dams, and not near where the ballroom was. One of the remaining towers crumbled beneath its former image and sank into the waters. The dragons had long flown off, and the fireballs had ceased. Though the immediate danger was over, I couldn't seem to relax myself to take stock of the situation. I stared towards the palace. The next thing I knew, I was one with the wailing citizens.

Drake. No...

I laid there, sprawled out on the ground, unsure of where to go from here. I *had* to find Drake, but I couldn't search the second largest city in the world while it was under a lake of water. I stood up. The sun was rising from behind the remains of the palace. The sky turned a bright pink, and then orange, and then finally yellow. The screaming had stopped, leaving only the stifled sobs of those who remained, until finally, the only sounds left were the flow of the water.

I sat up, I disgusted myself with my own stagnation, to stop moving is to allow death to take you, to stop breathing is to stop thinking, I had been lying here long enough. I looked at the tattered remains of my dress—it was torn from the knee down on one side. The slip for my right leg was just a hole. My hair had fallen from my bun and just hung above my shoulders. I had one heel left. I kicked off my shoe. No need for that anymore.

I stood there, in silence, for what felt like ages. I had no idea what to do. I never felt like this.

Clueless.

Helpless.

Marooned.

I reached for the scar on my cheek, It was sore but seemed to have stopped bleeding. I walked to the edge of the rooftop and looked. The water was clear. I could see the corpses below—the miscellaneous items floating. *Frozen* in time. *Preserved.* What was once labeled "*The greatest city in the world.*"

Flooded.

I wiped my sweaty hands on my dress, and I caught a glance at the ring Drake had given me. The next thing I knew, his words were echoing in my mind.

"*You make me brave. And I want to be brave.*"

I took a deep breath and turned to the wall of Lolem that remained intact, holding the water in.

"Perfect," I mumbled to myself.

I ran and dove into the water, swimming towards the wall. Luckily, the water was close to the same height as the wall, so I could climb up to the ledge with *little* to no problems. I got up and sat with my back against the ledge.

I turned to find a man—a guard, no less—weeping like a child.

I approached slowly, but he didn't react. As if he didn't see me. I touched his shoulder, and he panicked and crawled backward away, letting out a scream.

I pulled my hand back.

"*Are you alright?*" I asked, trying to comfort him.

The guard let out a shudder and nodded, tears streaking down his face.

"The… they all… *left*… someone *attacked*… and they *all... left*… to protect their *homes*… and I… *couldn't*…" he took a shuddering breath. "*I couldn't do it. The explosions happened—people screaming, crying. All I could do was curl up in a ball and whimper... My friends went to guard our home. They're brave. Me? I'm not brave...*" He slowly turned his head to me. He couldn't have been more than twenty. He wasn't as old as most soldiers; we seemed close in age.

"I have… *no*… I *had*… a *family.* A wife. A kid. And I didn't rush to them. I sat and cried. I'm *pathetic...*" He slammed his fists into his forehead. "*PATHETIC!!*" He proceeded to cry.

I grabbed one of his wrists.

"I need to release the water, and you can help. We'll find them together," I said. I tried to be as gentle but firm as I could—he was clearly in shock.

The man ripped his wrist from my grasp and slammed it to his forehead.

"*I'M NOT BRAVE. I CAN'T! I DON'T WANT TO DIE!*" His eyes welled up with tears.

I knelt down and laid a hand on his knee.

"I need your help. *Please*," I said, as I grabbed his chin and turned his face toward mine. "You *can* be brave. I need to blow the wall and release the water. We *can* find your family. I *promise*."

I tried to be persuasive. I thought I had failed.

But then the guard began to nod and stand up. He wiped his face and turned to me.

"We'll find them *together*. We'll drain the water, and we'll find them." I reassured him.

His voice wavered like a scared little kid, but he put on his helm and sheathed his sword.

The guard introduced himself as Ryan and led me towards a tower standing on the far edge of the city.

"There are towers built to get us off the wall in case of a flood—to make sure someone can inform Lord Roldan," he said.

I shook my head at his explanation. “I don’t know Roldan. There’s Verath, Dendrin, Rostov, Camilla and Cilmair, but no Roldan.” I listed off the lords I knew held kingdoms of Rhova.

Ryan stopped at a door and looked at me.

“Roldan is the lord of Kishak, the region beyond the blessed walls of Rhín. It’s the largest kingdom known to man. He isn’t known by many, so I’m not surprised by your disbelief.”

Ryan gave a light smile before unlocking the door and letting me go in first. “How are the walls blessed?” I asked curiously, Ryan shrugged and glanced off into the sprawling countryside of Calís. “The blessed walls of Rhín, are said to ward off mystics in Kishak; they may enter but cannot exit the kingdom after entry, some speculate they are the reason we don't see more mystics exhibiting magical abilities.” I nodded along with his words, mysticism was indeed rare, in all my years I had only encountered Drake.

I quickly descended the steps, the stone freezing my damp bare feet. I descended five flights and finally reached the ground floor. I found a group of men—more guards, four or five of them. They all raised their swords. Some had muskets and revolvers.

"*HALT!*" one of them shouted, shoving me into the wall and holding his blade to my neck.

I put my hands up in an attempt to calm them down. Ryan descended and attempted to talk them down.

"HEY! SHE'S WITH ME!" Ryan screamed as he pushed the man away from me and pulled his sword. They stood there, each ready to swing.

"*Ryan?*" one of the men asked.

They all slowly lowered their weapons—except for the one Ryan had shoved.

"Hey, Jack. She's a friend. Lower the blade."

Jack scowled at Ryan and began to swing. I charged and kicked him in the groin. He dropped his sword. I grabbed it and stepped back. The soldiers didn't flinch—except Jack, who fell to the ground like a sack of potatoes.

I stood tall, trying not to show that kicking his armor hurt like *hell*.

Jack cursed and shouted, but the other soldiers hugged and embraced Ryan.

"What *happened*? I thought you guys were running for the palace?" Ryan asked with a smile of relief.

"We were, but the flood caused debris to block the door in that direction. And the door to the outer wall is jammed, so we've been stuck here."

Jack stood up and began to stomp toward me. I pushed him into the wall and held the sword to his neck.

"*Uh-uh*, asshole. You'll sit your ass down or die trying," I said, maintaining my gaze with the group only gesturing with the blade.

The other soldiers backed up, including Ryan.

Jack just scowled, then he spit in my face. I leaped into action ready to end his journey here and now.

Ryan pulled me off him, as I ran for Jack.

"I have had one *hell* of a night, *don't test me!*" I shouted, but my voice went hoarse.

Jack scoffed and leaned against the wall. I took a deep breath and stepped back, until Ryan let me go.

Ryan explained to the men what we were planning to do, and they all seemed to disagree with it.

"Wouldn't that just flood the countryside?" one asked.

"No, *dumbass*. There are no walls to contain it—it would flow off into the bay," explained another.

"I don't care as long as we get rid of the water," said the last one.

Jack just rolled his eyes at us all.

"*Idiots. All of you,*" he said.

Ryan growled. "*DO YOU HAVE A BETTER IDEA, SMART GUY?*" he yelled.

Jack nodded. "*Yeah*. We need to get out of here to do that," he said with a cocky smile.

Ryan let out an angry exhale and slammed himself into the jammed door. Repeatedly like a wild animal.

It didn't budge.

"Well, nothing happened—except now I have internal bleeding," he said as he gripped his shoulder and winced.

"What if we do it two at a time?" one of the men suggested.

We all nodded. It's not a bad idea, to be completely honest.

Jack and Ryan decided to go first, going three times before quitting.

"Damn it, that hurt," Jack exclaimed, rubbing his arm.

"I literally just said that *asshole*," Ryan retorted.

Jack looked at Ryan and said, "Yeah, *I know*. But I mean—you're not a *real* man, so what would you know about pain?"

Jack gave a chuckle, but Ryan just glared daggers at him.

I stepped up to the door next.

All the men spoke up.

"What makes you think you can do more than those guys did?" one of them asked.

I scoffed and pulled Ryan up. Together, we charged—and the door swung open. Together, we fell to the ground.

I stood up and pulled Ryan up. The soldiers scoffed and ran off toward the gate.

I looked at Ryan. "You were brave in there. You're hardly pathetic," I said with a genuine smile, and ran after the group.

The closer we got to the gate, the soggier the ground got. It was intact but leaking little streams of water near the center but held strong.

“So? We just blow up the gate?” one man asked.

Jack nodded and approached the giant gate. “But *how?*” he asked.

“Explosives?” I asked.

All the men shook their heads.

“Inside—probably too damp to use,” one said.

“Other villages?” I asked, looking toward Calís.

The men shrugged collectively at a loss.

“How about opening the gate? How would one do that?” I asked.

Ryan looked at me. “There are levers on the upper wall, in case of flooding. They’re used in emergencies!” he added enthusiastically.

He turned and dashed to the tower we had emerged from.

I hesitated—then turned and followed him.

I got in the door, and Ryan was upstairs already. I followed. I could hear his footsteps, but he never came back into view—until I got to the top. He dashed to the levers, which stood just above the gate. He opened two small hatches and told me to pull one on his count.

One.
Two.
Three.

The gate began to burst into life, and water began to rush out of the gate. The men ran to get out of the way—but one wasn't fast enough. He got pushed all the way off the cliff, into the bay.

On the bright side, the city was draining.

Now to find Drake.

Act II: He Walked Beside Me Once

"*MARIA! CLEA! I'M COMING FOR YOU*!" Ryan shouted as he sprinted to the tower stairwell. I followed not far behind.

We went all the way back to the gate and met back up with the group. We all walked the water-soaked streets of Lolem—pale, bloated corpses littered the streets. What was left of the celebration was scattered about as well.

Ryan dashed ahead, searching corpses as he went. People eventually emerged from some of the tallest buildings and joined our group. Eventually, we gained a group of a hundred or so survivors. Lolem was known for having a population in the thousands in the past. This was nothing compared to that.

Deep down, I wanted to go search for Drake, but I promised Ryan we'd look for his family. So, I kept a level head for him. I ran ahead and helped him search the corpses.

He turned the corner and stopped cold in his tracks.

"Ryan?" I asked. I walked up behind him and caught a glimpse of what he was looking at. It was a young woman, clinging to a support beam holding up a deck. It looked like this was where she was when the dam burst and the waves tried to pull her away, but she held firm. She was frozen to the spot.

Ryan let out a gasp and ran to peel her off the beam.

"DON'T JUST STAND THERE! HELP ME!" he shouted.

The group just watched and murmured to themselves quietly. I approached and tried to peel her fingers off the beam—she was frozen solid. This was bringing the statement "death grip" into a literal sense. We were *finally* able to get her free and laid her flat the best we could.

Ryan knelt over Maria's corpse and sobbed into her chest, mumbling something under his breath. He wiped his face, stood up, and ran into the house.

"*CLEA!*" he shouted. "*CLEA!!*"

I walked into the house and up the stairs after Ryan. He ran into a bedroom with scattered stuffed toys and then frantically ran up another set of stairs. I followed. Halfway up, I heard Ryan gasp again.

I climbed up and joined Ryan in the attic, staring at a little girl playing quietly with her dolls on the floor.

The attic floor was damp, so this room was indeed underwater, but she was more than alive. Ryan ran ahead and wrapped Clea in a tight hug.

"Oh. Hi, Daddy," she gave out a giggle.

Ryan began to kiss her cheeks frivolously. "THANK THE GODS!" He grabbed Clea by the hand and led her out to the street.

I gave a smile. I'm happy for him. But now it's my turn.

I ran out to the street like my life depended on it and sprinted for the palace.

"*DRAKE!*" I screamed. Ryan picked up his pace carrying Clea and ran to keep up with me.

I climbed the first set of stairs, cut through the courtyard, then the final set of stairs. The drawbridge was up.

I turned to Ryan. "How do we raise it?" I asked.

He shook his head. "I work the wall… I don't know."

I groaned and walked along the edge just before the moat and looked for a way in. A window, something. I grabbed a flag out of the ground and threw it at the closest window like a javelin. The glass shattered and water began to flow out.

I took a few steps back, ran full speed, and jumped, just barely catching a grip on the windowsill.

I held a firm grip on the ledge—glass piercing my hand—I let out a shriek and pulled myself up enough to climb through. I fell to the ground and laid there. spent.

"*Are you alright?!*" Ryan asked from outside.

"Yeah. I'm good!" I yelled back, I got no verbal response he heard me, I ripped off a strip of my dress and wrapped it around my bloody hand.

I turned and looked around the door. There had to be a lever for the drawbridge.

As I was searching, there was a scream echoing through the halls. It was a woman. I ran up the steps and down the left corridor at the top.

I ran past the waterlogged decor looking for the source of the scream. I came upon a throne room with a crack in the door. I opened it a little more and peeked in.

It was Queen Cilmair, knelt down in a guillotine, and Verath stood above her with his hand on the rope. She was desperately pleading with her captor.

"*PLEASE*, DON'T DO THIS! WE HAD A *DEAL*!" she pleaded.

"WE *HAD* A DEAL WHEN IT INVOLVED THE KINGDOM BEING INTACT. OBVIOUSLY, ROLDAN KNOWS MY PRESENCE UNDER YOUR BANNER!" Verath bellowed, his voice cracked with fury as he yelled in her direction.

Cilmair sobbed. "I didn't tell him… I swear… PLEASE DON'T DO THIS…"

Before she could continue her wailing, Verath yanked the cord and the blade dropped, ripping her head clean from her body.

"*Next*." Verath's tone was calm, almost bored.

A soldier dressed in Lolem's symbol led a man in a tuxedo with a burlap sack over his head into Cilmair's place. Verath ripped off the sack with a dramatic flourish and threw it aside.

He gave a chuckle. "How are you doing, Phoenix? Your lady abandon you yet?"

Drake! I was so relieved.

Verath's tone sounded lighter than it did with Cilmair. I have to stop him before he tries to kill Drake.

I gripped the hilt of Jack's sword and readied myself to charge into the room.

Drake looked up to Verath. "Actually, the opposite. *I was an ass,* and now I may not see her again." Drake gave a saddened smile and looked to the floor. "Just get it over with, just *please*… don't hurt Akira, *leave her alone*." he pleaded to Verath.

Verath knelt down and lifted Drake's head. "That seems to happen a lot with you two. You are *never* together at the same time, except the one time—you know? The time you *killed* my guys?" He gave a manic chuckle, his eye twitched erratically as he continued to cackle. "*Finally*. An eye for an eye." His sigh was one of great relief as if he had been carrying this weight for ages.

Maybe his tone wasn't nicer than it was with Cilmair.

I slammed the door open some more—and ran.

"*STOP!*" I shouted as I charged the guillotine. I readied my sword and went straight for Verath. One of the soldiers' shield-charged me and shoved me into a wall holding me firm in place. He continued to push me into it almost as if he was trying to crush me. I used the wall to my advantage—raised my legs up, and pushed him away, and rammed my sword through his throat. He stared at me in disbelief and collapsed to the floor.

I grabbed his shield and ran for Verath. "*Akira!*" Drake exclaimed in relief.

Verath stood up and gave out a laugh. I continued to run for him, "I'm so sorry Akira!" Tears streamed down Drake's face, but just as I was about to hit Verath, he rolled out of the way of my swing and ran toward the exit effectively pulling the cord. The blade fell in slow motion—and I watched in horror as it ripped Drake's head off.

My heart sank as I watched my husband's decapitated head roll into the basket.

A debilitating shock rolled through my body.

I fell to my knees and dropped everything in my grasp.

I cried out far louder than I ever imagined I could. I let out a scream so harrowing I thought I may deafen myself from it. I wailed until I couldn't anymore. I weakly grabbed Drake's head and held it in my lap.

I wiped the tears from my eyes and closed his eyes. "No… *no*… *no*… Please… I like me better when I'm with you…" I whimpered silently, almost like a prayer, hoping someone, anyone would answer my call.

I placed his head back in the basket. I placed a piece of cloth I found nearby over the basket and lifted it. I carried the basket back to the door. The soldiers stood at attention and ignored me as I showed myself out.

The drawbridge had been lowered, somehow. I carried the basket across the bridge and placed it on the ground. I turned back around and headed back toward the throne room.

"What is *that? ... Where are you going? ... Akira...?*" Ryan asked curiously.

Clea peeked in the basket and screamed, "*DADDY!*" She began to sob.

Ryan rocked her and shushed her to calm her down. I climbed the stairs at a slow pace.

I will not leave him here.

Ryan ran up behind me as I approached the throne room.

"*Akira? What the hell is wrong with you?*" He passed me and stood in front of the doorway. He looked me in the eye. "*WHAT IS WRONG WITH YOU?*" he asked firmly.

My eyes began to twitch. I thrust my knee into his stomach with full force. He fell to the ground.

I stumbled into the room and laid Drake's decapitated corpse flat on the ground. I dragged him by his feet. I struggled to pull my breaths into my body. Tears seemed to keep my face wet with the constant streams.

Ryan groaned and stood up. "*WAIT! WAIT!*" He walked over and ripped down some drapes. "*We can drag him better with this,*" he said in a low sorrowful voice.

I sighed and knelt down by Drake's neck. Sniffling as I lifted his upper body enough to get the sheet under. Ryan did the same. We carried him down the hallway and eventually the stairs without any further issue.

I laid the sheet down on the drawbridge and walked down the stairs.

"*Where are you going...?*" Ryan asked, his voice seemed to echo around me, as if trying to find a way for me to hear his words.

I ignored him.

I proceeded down the stairs, through the courtyard, and down the next staircase. I walked down the street for what seemed like an eternity, all the way to the stable. I grabbed a small wheelbarrow and emptied it of the waterlogged hay, then started to wheel it up the hill.

People stopped to ask if I needed help. I just continued on my way.

I will not leave him here.

I cannot leave him here.

I got the wheelbarrow to the lowest step of stairs below the courtyard. I returned to Drake and grabbed his head and walked it down first. I then carried the body with help from Ryan.

"*You're not going to pull that yourself, are you?*"

I readied Drake, then grabbed the handles and pulled the wheelbarrow downhill, maintaining a slow speed. My tears fell to the drenched marble streets, mixing with the sorrow of the last 24 hours.

I had a bad feeling about this—and we came *anyway.*

Ryan kept my speed and continued asking me questions.

"*Are you going to say anything? Anything at all…?*"

I heard his words, but my brain had shut down all outside communication.

I wasn't there anymore.

I felt hollow, like I was watching my body go on without me. I was focused on one objective.

I cannot leave him here.

I tried to think of a reply for Ryan, but my mind just kept replaying the sound of the blade falling. ***Whoooooshing.***

The sight of his head falling into the basket.

I turned to Ryan, with tearful eyes. "The man… I love… died… *he... died...*" I almost crumbled to my knees again, Ryan moved to catch me, but I steadied myself. I took a shallow breath and turned back to the road ahead.

That's what's left.

The road ahead.

I cannot leave him here.

Whoooooshing.

He died...?

No…?

The road ahead...

What do I do now…?

I blinked back my tears; I was enraged by the fact the tears continued despite me repeatedly wiping my face.

Whoooooshing.

The thought of him gone…*hurt*…

I felt pain.

I miss you…

I'm afraid to be alone again…

No… no…

I need you…

I walked through the gate and followed the dirt path that led me to the horizon.

No destination in mind.

Just my thoughts circling around each other, warping together. One thought dominated them all:

I cannot leave him here.

Chapter 27: Let the World Watch Him Grieve

Act I: "Fine—Tell Me What Comes Next"

The room stank of old wood and dying light.

I sat on the floor, knees bent to my chest, cowering like a child, my back against a wall that hadn't been cleaned in years. Dust stirred with every shallow breath I released. The room filled with a circle of mirrors, all beaten and battered, and covered in shape or form.

Only one mirror remained uncovered. The rest were forcibly silenced.

Cracked. Crooked. Its silvering had a warped and distorted persuasion to its words, leaving a jagged bloom across its center like a wound refusing to heal.

I stared at it without blinking. Listening intently to its words.

"*You look pathetic,*" my reflection said. I didn't know why, but despite its demeanor, I remained in my spot.

I didn't flinch; I was used to harsh words by now.

"I thought you'd be gone by now." I said meekly, "I'm a lost cause, a joke. Not worth my weight in gold." my eyes betrayed me and tossed some tears down my cheeks as my voice filled the air.

The spirit-version of me stepped from the edge of the glass—same eyes, same jaw, same voice. But *cleaner. More polished. Crueler.*

"I don't go anywhere," My reflection said. "You just keep looking away." He said with a sinister smile.

I swallowed harshly. My knuckles were still raw from Lolem's alleys, for a moment I thought I was hallucinating again, the voices never ceased, not even my own. Filling my thoughts with horrific obscenities.

"She's out there," I muttered softly. "*Commanding. Grieving. Playing queen of the ashes, she made.*" My bloody fists met the sides of my head gripping wads of hair as I rocked in place.

"*Grieving,*" the spirit scoffed. "As if she's the one who lost everything." He walked over and attempted to meet my gaze. His firm grasp met my chin, lifting my eyes to his.

"She always wins," I said, voice low. "Even when the world burns." My eye twitched for what seemed like forever, I slammed my clenched fists into my eye sockets. "*WHY WON'T THIS STOP!*" I screeched.

"She didn't win." My reflection stated firmly.

"*She always does!*" I shouted, tears welled in my eyes, until they burned my cool cheeks.

"She *outlasts*," the reflection corrected. "*That's different.*"

My eyes narrowed. "*You sound like you admire her.*" I felt pins of rage on the back of my neck, MY *REFLECTION*— Siding with the enemy, PATHETIC!

The spirit sneered. "I *loathe* her. But we learn from what we hate."

He began circling the room slowly, his boots silent on the old wood, letting out the quietest groan to his authority.

"You've raged. You've bled. You've howled like an animal. And *still*—she walks. That should tell you something."

I leaned forward, elbows on my knees. "Tell me *what*?"

"That she's not *unbreakable*. Just better at hiding the cracks. Maybe the problem is you."

Silence filled the room like a bloated corpse.

"I don't want her *broken,*" I said. "I want her *gone.*" I seethed through clenched teeth.

The reflection smiled, the edges of his mouth slowly reaching for his eyes, sharp as flint.

“Then stop screaming.” He ordered.

He crouched beside me, gripping my face, harsher this time, his inches from mine.

“Stop running.”

“Stop begging ghosts to love you back.”

“And start becoming the thing she fears.”

My jaw tightened. The air buzzed with something like static—like lightning that hadn't been able to strike.

“I don’t have a plan,” I said weakly, tears continuing to stream down my face.

“Then steal one.” He spoke sharp and clear like light fragmenting of a crystal tumbler.

“I don’t have allies.” I pleaded.

“Then pretend you do.” He scoffed harshly.

“I don’t know who I am anymore.” I wailed.

The reflection's eyes flashed. He whispered like a knife sliding into a sheath.

"You are what she made you when she couldn't kill you too. You're both weak, made for each other frankly." He gave a dramatic whoosh of his cloak when he turned away.

And then he was gone.

The mirror showed only me.

Bloody. Bruised. Alone.

A scared child in the boots of a man.

Playing pretend.

I stood slowly. Back stiff. Breath shallow.
And in the empty room with dust and silence and battlefield of cracked mirrors, I whispered:
"*Then let's give her something to fear.*"

Act II: Festival For the Fallen

The room smelled like polish and rot.

I sat alone at the long council table, my fingers tapping the wood in erratic patterns. Stained glass spilled fractured light across the marble, painting me in colors that didn't belong to a monster like me.

"She took the *moon*," I murmured softly. "Took her man. Took the godsdamned stage." my voice no longer sounded like mine.

From the shadows wailing silently onto the floor near the fireplace, my reflection paced. One emerged among the broken.

"Poor, pitiful you," he drawled. "You lost one little eclipse and now you want to throw a fucking party."

I didn't look at him. "It's *not* a *celebration.*"

"No," the spirit scoffed. "It's a tomb with paper lanterns." He rolled his eyes and propped his head up in his hand like he was bored of my stupidity.

"I'm giving them something to mourn with." I said eagerly.

"You're giving them something to distract them from the fact that you were dragged through the dirt like a mad dog." He shot back.

I stood abruptly, caught off guard by his honesty.

I walked to the towering window and looked down at Lolem's broken plaza. The tower shadows filled the once prosperous city with a devastating smog. The scorched banners were still being pulled from the walls.

"They'll gather," I said confidently. "They'll cry. And then they'll look for someone to thank."

The spirit leaned against the wall next to the window, grinning to me.

"Right. Because when people are grieving and scared, what they really want is a eulogy from a lunatic who murders girls in public."

My jaw clenched.

"You're not real." I said with my eyes closed hoping that I could will him away.

"I'm more real than whatever the hell you are now." He said in a confident voice.

I turned. Fast. Until we stood face to face, somehow, despite us being the same person, he stood a confident foot above me.

"I *must* do *something*. I *have to matter*." I pleaded with a furious smack to my twitching eye.

He laughed.

Low. Cruel. Sinister.

"You think she's watching you from whatever ash pile she's crying in?"

I flinched. The air pulsed like static.

"She *ruined* you," he hissed. "And now you want to throw a funeral with your name on the flier like it's going to make the world forget how pathetic you looked—bleeding in the street, begging ghosts to say your name."

I grabbed a quill. Slammed it to parchment.

Festival of Remembrance.

The spirit snorted. "Sounds *holy.*"

"*Shut up*." I snapped.

"A night of reflection and peace."

"She'll laugh when she hears about it. You know that, right?"

"For the fallen," I whispered. "Not for her. *Never* for her."

The spirit walked behind me. Leaned in. Whispered right in my ear:

"Then make it *hurt.*"

I paused, thinking until I let the words settle.

Then smiled.

"It's not a trap," I said softly. "It's a sermon."

"*For my dear friend, Drake.*"

Chapter 28: The Pursuit of Peace

Act I: I Buried My World, With Him

I walked along the faded paths of Calís. Some people tried to convince me to come out of the rain, take a break. I had no intention of stopping. I just kept pulling the wheelbarrow. I hadn't begun to feel tired, or hungry. I felt nothing. I just continued walking.

Ryan rode up on a horse a little while after. He kicked over my wheelbarrow and snapped his fingers in my face. "*SNAP OUT OF IT, AKIRA!*" His words echoed violently, as if he was in the distance, shouting from a mile away.

He gripped my shoulders and shook me frantically. "*AKIRA!*" Thunder struck nearby as he yelled, as if the gods agreed with the suggestion.

I broke from his grasp and slammed him into the ground with only my shoulder. I picked up my wheelbarrow and replaced Drake inside and continued on our way. Ryan ran ahead of me and blocked my path.
"*You cannot go through this alone. You can punch me, kick me, beat me all you want, but you cannot do this by yourself.*" His words echoed but held a pleading tone.

There we stood in the pouring rain, at an impasse. I looked him in the eye and did my best to make sure he heard me.

"*Leave. Me. Alone.*"
I gripped the wheelbarrow and started to walk. The closer I got to Sylhalin, I noticed Atlas following behind me, a quiet shadow in silver-stained armor, his paws near-silent on the wet ground.

Ryan didn't follow me after that. I just walked to Sylhalin in silence.

"*Someone at the gate!*"
"Raise the gate, it's the queen!"
"You look like hell. What happened?"

I walked through the city and ignored the stares. I dragged the wheelbarrow up the streets toward the northern outskirts. I decided I was going to take him to the end of the road. I dragged him for hours. The rain let up about halfway through my journey there.

I finally reached the edge of Sylhalin, the end of walls, roads, and civilization. I let go of the handles and walked the short path to the cottage. I walked in and picked up the bottle of wine off the bedside table.

I saw the ruffled bedsheets we had left early yesterday morning.

"*My Gods, I love you, you know that?*" Drake's voice echoed in my ears. I could see his goofy smile in my mind; I scowled at the bed in fury.

Why didn't I say it back? He deserved better. I turned and left the cottage without a word. I walked back to Drake. I grabbed the handles and dragged him towards where we had our picnic.

I sat in the grass and opened the bottle.
"Cheers, to being alone, yet again."
I took a swig and smashed it on the wheelbarrow. Glass showering the joyous spot we had left

I proceeded to punch and kick the wheelbarrow. I'll admit, part of me blamed him for storming off. Getting himself killed, I knew it was a bad idea, and I allowed us to go, so I too held blame.

Atlas stayed nearby, laying in the grass with his ears low, silent and solemn.

I sat there, watching the ships sail through the bay. After a while I got sick of sitting. I wandered the cottage grounds. I eventually found a rusted old shovel and began to dig a hole where the blanket was, right where our picnic had been.

It took me hours, but I managed to get a hole dug just before dark. I lowered Drake into the hole and covered him with the sheet. I began to fill the hole.

"Akira?"

I turned in search of the voice calling to me. I turned to see Ryan approaching me from the road. Walking alongside him was Clea.

I rolled my eyes.
"*Great*, here to rub your miracle in some *more*?"
I tried to keep my tone cold and sharp—it was my intention to hurt him enough verbally to leave me alone.

"*No. We're here to make sure you get through this,*" he said.

I scoffed at his words and continued to fill the grave.

All I had to do was save him. Be quick enough to get him out of there alive. But no, I wasn't.

I was too late.
"TOO LATE!" I screamed as I threw the shovel into the ocean and climbed out of the hole, charging to the cottage.

Ryan stood there, at the head of the grave I had dug, watching me leave. Atlas rose, his armor faintly rattling as he stepped between Ryan and the grave, a low growl warning him not to follow.

I sighed and turned around.
"What do you want?" I asked in a low, impatient voice.

"I am here for you. You don't want empathy, you don't want company, but you will want something eventually. I'm here. I'm your man," he said calmly.

I walked toward him. Within arm's length. I locked eyes with him. I gave a gentle smile—
—and then proceeded to spit on his armor.

I turned and walked to the cottage. I slammed the door as hard as I could and threw a chair at the wall. I was about to lie down on the bed, but I couldn't bring myself to disturb the mess we left.

Together.

I opened the closet and pulled out extra bedding. I built a makeshift bed in front of the fireplace and found myself sleeping. Atlas sat by the door, unmoving, silent, watching.

I woke up to Ryan lighting candles in the kitchen, and Clea reading a book on the bed. I immediately got up and pushed her off the bed. I frantically tried to restore what she had disturbed.

"WHAT WERE YOU THINKING?!" I shouted. She sat on the floor and cried. Ryan helped her up and sat her at the kitchen table, not paying me any attention. "*Gods, I just love you—*" Drake's voice echoed in my skull, and I began to cry again.

“Beef stew?” Ryan asked, filling three bowls at the table.

I huffed.
“Why can’t you just leave me alone, *you repulsive freak*? I don’t want your help, nor do I need your help. *LEAVE. ME. ALONE.*” The hot tears burned my cheeks, I was filled with rage, I thought I’d melt through the floor.

I marched to the door and slammed it as hard as I could. I took to the road and walked back. I turned and avoided town—the last thing I needed was to be gawked at some more. Or God forbid, *helped*.

I walked until I reached the western wall of Sylhalin. I walked through the guard tower and came out in the Sarnawenian Forests. I wandered south for a bit, in a forest just west of what used to be Rostov’s camp.

I walked through the forest. The canopy began to close the deeper I went. The air became thick. I continued to trek through the smog until I collapsed. The last thing I remembered was being picked up by a tree.

Finally, *Death.*

—

The next thing I remembered was the firm grasp around me. Tightening as it held me in place.

"*What the hell is it holding?*" a man asked.
"*How would I know, Zane?*" another said.

I let out a groan. This thing was squeezing me tighter.
"*It's a woman, Zane! Charge it!*"

I groaned some more. These guys were not making this tree any happier.
OW. HOLY HELL.

I struggled to open one eye. The one man slashed the tree's arm—three quick swipes—and I fell to the ground. The other dragged me back. I watched as the first continued to fight the tree, then did a backflip toward us.

They both began reciting some sort of mantra. Not long after, a shimmering ward glowed as it rose above us and prevented the tree from hitting us.

The man knelt beside me.
"Hello, I'm Takka and this is Zane. What's your name?"

Zane continued reciting the mantra, keeping the tree at bay.

I furrowed my brow and tried to stand.
"Woah, woah, woah. You shouldn't try to stand up. You're weak. You should rest."

Takka seemed to believe what he was saying. I scoffed and stood up.
"You should've let it kill me," I mumbled.

Takka began reciting the mantra again. A ward shimmered as it appeared around me. He waved a finger back and forth as I attempted to leave.
I slammed on the Dome in fury.

As I watched Zane fight the tree—its limbs becoming twisted mockeries of arms and legs—I felt my breath catch.

I remembered—

The first time I fought one of these things.
A gnarled tree. Cold wind. My katana drawn, hand trembling. My boots slipping in the mud.

"Why were you in a tree?" I'd said then, heart pounding.
"I'm so sorry, Akira!" Drake's sorrowful voice filled every crevice in my mind.

"What are you looking at?!" I snapped.
"Just watching your face furrow. You know I love it. But don't take life so seriously!" Drake said with a playful chuckle.

His voice spun around me. I forced my hand to my chest.

Zane slashed his sword through the tree and the force of the tree disintegrating threw him into Takka's barrier.

Takka knelt over his friend, attempting to wake him. A woman rose from the tree's ashes. She gripped her head and approached the clerics.
"What happened...?" She asked.

What the hell? She emerged from the tree... like... Drake.

Takka ignored her, continuing to pray for the shield encasing me.

I slammed my fists against the dome, but I doubt my words escaped.

The woman stood around my height, about average. Platinum blonde hair and blue eyes. She wore tattered clothes unlike the clerics. I couldn't judge for myself—my gown had been ripped to hell over the past couple days.

Takka stopped reciting the mantra and the shield fell away. I turned and stormed away, but I didn't get far before I fell unconscious again.

"I'll get her," I heard Takka say.
"Would you get him please?" he asked the woman.
She gave a verbal agreement.

I just want to be left alone.

Alone.
Please, God. Leave me alone.

Act II: So, This Is How the World Unravels

"She hasn't eaten in days. She hasn't moved. She just lies there, staring out the window. She's a waste of effort." It was a man's voice. He sounded upset.

"I couldn't just leave her out there, Zane" Another man chimed in.

"So, let me just get this straight—you two are clerics? This woman isn't a friend of yours? So do you make a habit of bringing home random women?" a woman asked.

"...No?" both men retorted.

There was a click of a door opening. The woman with platinum blonde hair walked into view and knelt down in front of me.
"You need to eat," she said, as she set a plate of random food on the bedstand. She moved her face into my eyeline, then waved her hand in front of my face. She let out a sigh and walked back towards the door.

"She's not doing well. She won't last much longer if she doesn't eat something." The woman let out a sigh and closed the door.

"I don't know what we're going to do with her," one man said.

"That's a pretty formal gown. Or at least it was before she destroyed it," the woman stated.
"You think she was at a party of some sort?" one of the men asked.

"Maybe she was at the Lunar Eclipse Festival in Lolem. I heard someone attacked minutes before the eclipse." one man said with his mouth full.

The woman sighed. *"I wonder what happened to make her like this."*

"Did you hear that Lolem was flooded? The ambush destroyed the dam—killed everyone in the lower levels." The man sounded almost enthused, like he had witnessed it happen.

The other man let out a laugh. *"No way. Lolem has been a pillar of peace since the First Age. There's no way it fell in the matter of hours to an unknown assailant. They have one of the best armies in the world."*

He wasn't wrong. They had been the strongest kingdom for decades.
But it did indeed fall. I watched it breathe its last breath.

I sat there listening. The walls were thin—I heard their conversation, not much else.
I looked to the pillow to my right, then lay back down and stared at the ceiling.

I closed my eyes.
I was tired.
So *tired.*

I woke up to Drake watching me sleep.
He let out a laugh and smiled.

"How long have you been staring at me sleep?" I asked, trying not to laugh.

He shook his head. "Not long," he said with a chuckle.

I looked around and noticed I wasn't in the same room.
I was back in the cottage.

I sat up. "Is this a dream?"

Drake stood up and looked at me, confused.
"How do you mean?"

I stood up and looked out the window—it looked just how it should. The field of grass, the blue sky, the ocean going to the horizon, holding up the icebergs.
"This is a dream? This is my brain trying to make me feel better."

Drake gave a heavy laugh. "Have you gone mad?" He poured himself a glass of wine.

"Maybe I have gone mad," I said under my breath.

I stepped away from the window and walked to the kitchen table. I took a seat. Drake walked to the counter and set a bowl of soup on the table in front of me.
"You should eat," he said, taking a seat next to me.

I pushed it away. "I'm fine."

He got up and took the bowl. He grabbed a plate with meat, set it down in front of me, and then I saw—it was steak.

"I don't care if you're fine. I said eat," he said in an authoritative tone.

I rolled my eyes and took a bite. "Happy?" I said mid-chew.
He nodded in approval. He took a sip of his wine and walked to the bed. He set it on the bedstand and lied down.

I blinked—and the next thing I knew, I was back in bed. Drake looked at me, holding up his head with his arm as he lay facing me.

"The perfect way to celebrate our wedding is to go to the Lunar Eclipse Festival in Lolem. It'll be a nice change of pace—no killing, no life-or-death decisions. Just an elegant night of food and all of the liquor you can drink."

I shook my head. "That's not a good idea. No," I replied. I stood up, but the next thing I knew I was back in bed, and Drake was still in the same pose.

"Good morning. How'd you sleep?" he asked.

A shiver went down my spine.

"Fine. I slept fine." I said, trying and failing to hide my unease.

I stood up and went for my armor and sword, but it all blew away like dust before I could reach it. I looked out the window—and the fields of grass, the ocean, and the sky all began to blow away like the seeds of a dandelion.

I ran for the door. Drake appeared and placed a hand on it, leaning against it.
I backed away.
I have gone mad.
I must have.
That's the only explanation.

Drake smiled. But the door began to disappear. Eventually, he wasn't leaning against it. His hand started to vaporize—but he didn't react. He just kept eye contact. He opened his mouth to speak—but he began to disappear.

Before I knew it, the cottage was gone.

I was surrounded by nothing.
Nothing at all.

I spun in all directions.
Nothing.
Nothing at all.

I was alone.
I ran in a random direction, bolting as fast as I could.

My surroundings didn't seem to change—but that didn't stop me. I kept running. Looking for a place to go. Anywhere at all.

I stopped abruptly.
I tried to catch my balance—but I was too late. I fell.
I let out a scream, but nothing came out.
I fell into an abyss of darkness.
I fell for what felt like eternity—until I slammed into the ground.

I let out a groan. I lied there letting my body throb and ache.
Pain—everywhere.

"Greetings."

I looked around weakly—but didn't get up.
I looked up. Standing above me was a man in a white trench coat. He had medium-length black hair and blue

eyes. His eyes seemed to change between different hues of blue. Six sets of wings flowed from his back, fluttering slightly almost like a skittish animal's tail. It was breathtaking, nonetheless.

He extended a hand. I took it. He pulled me up. I wiped myself off—I still felt dirty.

The man gave me a thin smile.
"Welcome to limbo," he said in a calm tone.

A chill ran through me. Limbo? It didn't make sense. Was this death? Was I dreaming? I wanted to ask—but my voice didn't come.

I blinked a few times in confusion.
"Limbo?" I asked, my voice broke telling anyone who had heard me, I'd been overusing it.

The man gave a nod.
"Isn't it great? It's my favorite afterlife. So much possibility." He gave a satisfied sigh.

I looked around. All I saw was pitch black darkness in all areas.
"I'm sorry—afterlife? I'm not dead," I said.

The man looked at me. His face had changed—he took on a serious look.
"No. But you will be soon."

His words echoed around me. They seemed to fill the darkness surrounding me, serving as a terrifying landscape.

Chapter 29: A Close Call

Act I: Where the Bells Only Ring Once

I began to laugh, almost uncontrollably.

The man kept the same serious look on his face. He seemed unamused, but I couldn't help myself. Me? Dead? The thought seemed far-fetched.

"Are you done? Because I only have so much time for this visit before you have no choice," he said, letting out a sigh as he turned away. He waved a hand for me to follow.

We walked through the darkness. I looked around for something—anything—but there was nothing. Just black. So dull.

"Choice? What choice?" I asked.

The man stopped in his tracks. "We'll get to that in a few minutes."

He reached a hand forward and turned it, as if twisting a doorknob. The darkness split open into a door-shaped passage. The man led me through. I walked in, and the door closed behind us. He poofed into existence ahead of me.

"Watch," he said.

We were back in the room I'd been in before falling asleep. The door flew open, and the woman with platinum-blonde hair walked to the window. She threw open the curtains, letting in a flood of light.

"Come on, up and at 'em," she said.

She walked over, tossed off the blanket, and sat me up in bed. I looked horrible. My eyes were sunken in their sockets, my hair clumped together, and I had a dead look on my face. I stared through her. She sighed.

"I wish I could do something to help you. But I can't if you don't accept it."

She sat beside me and placed a hand over mine. Then she stood and left the room.

I remained seated, staring out the window. But not for long.

I fell forward off the bed to the floor.

My face hit with a thud. I gasped.

"What just happened?" I asked the man in shock.

He looked at me. “Your heart stopped. Starvation put stress on your body, and the grief certainly didn’t help.”

“No… People don’t just die like that. I wouldn’t just die,” I sputtered.

“You did,” he said with eerie calm.

He walked over to a door and opened it. He motioned for me to follow, but I couldn’t stop staring at my body—still lying face-down on the floor, slowly cooling.

Reluctantly, I followed him.

We exited and ended up floating above the walls of Rhín. An army marched toward the gates.

“This is two weeks from today. Two weeks after *your passing*,” he said.

I watched as imperial troops lined the walls, firing flaming arrows down at the invaders. But the soldiers below raised their shields. The arrows bounced off. The crowd split, and a figure walked through the middle. It looked too large to be a man alone.

The man led me closer.

As we approached, I saw Verath, he had replaced his traditional stark blue cloak with a familiar bloody tiger-print cloak.

I gasped. "*Atlas…*" My heart shattered at the thought of him becoming a symbol of Verath, how horrific my poor cubs' final moments must've been.

"King Verath of Ciron after the fall of Lolem recaptured Sylhalin, and then Sarnawen. The kingdom was abandoned by its armies, and the civilians surrendered. Khofte was spared for being so isolated. That leaves Kishak—his *final* conquest."

He continued, "The imperial soldiers of Kishak held off the ambush. Lord Roldan ordered all able bodies in Rhova to serve the king. His men traveled the land, conscripting them by force. Verath's army was split in two—only the worthy, the pure, could enter the kingdom after the walls were once again blessed at the coronation."

"Coronation?" I asked.

He nodded, leading me toward the palace in the center of Kishak. The kingdom was massive, stretching for miles. Inside the palace sat a woman with long brown hair and porcelain features. She sat on the throne, examining her nails.

"*Queen Camilla of Sarnawen*, and soon to be of Rhova. If Verath falls, she stands to claim Ciron as well."

He led me to a courtyard decorated for the event. He snapped his fingers. Time skipped forward. The moon neared the center sky. The courtyard was full of terrified people. Camilla ascended the stairs to the stage and knelt before the crowd, who erupted in cheers. A man placed a golden crown on her head. She stood and bowed. The moon centered above her and released a gentle beam of light.

She inhaled deeply, looked up, and raised her hand elegantly.

She clenched her fist—and the moon began to tremble and quake.

Then it shattered.

The crowd erupted in immense panic as chunks of moon rock fell from the sky. In a thunderous voice, she shouted:

"*WHERE IS KING VERATH?*"

The man beside me spoke: "Camilla is the daughter of Lord Rotik, and another full-blooded mystic. With the coronation, she was divinely bound to the start of Armageddon if she stood in a seat of immense power—to cleanse the earth."

Moon rocks caught fire as they descended, gaining speed, Buildings collapsed as they collided. The ground split, spilling lava into the streets. Camilla levitated above the stage, her blue cloak billowing in the winds furious lashing. Verath approached with half the army he once had. The walls surrounding Kishak activated.

Verath closed his eyes, arms raised. When he reopened them, they glowed deep red. He released a purple orb of energy, with a wave of his hand, A crowd of figures appeared beside him. I recognized some faces—Sam, the loud paladin Drake had silenced. In a demonic voice, he bellowed:

"CHARGE! KILL THE QUEEN!"

His soldiers surged forward—but the ground crumbled beneath them. They vanished, then reappeared at his side. Camilla descended the regal marble staircase.

He swung his energy again and missed.

She raised a hand, clenched it, and lifted him off the ground by the throat.

"*You will bow to me—or perish!*" Her voice was shrill. She was done waiting.

"Never." Verath rasped.

She slammed him into the ground. It cracked beneath him. He fell into magma and vanished in the lava without another word.

I gasped.

The man snapped his fingers. Time froze. Camilla smiled into the magma. A purple aura wavered from the magma's surface and wafted towards Camilla, Her eyes glowed white. Like she was smelling a nostalgic smell from long ago.

The man accompanying me snapped his fingers again. Time jumped forward. Kishak lay in ruins. The palace was rebuilt—this time, with slaves and orcs flooding the palace grounds.

"She gained Verath's abilities," the man said. "She claimed his skills to raise spirits but combined with her affinity towards plant life she could raise corpses with plant life allowing her to control them individually at will as well."

Camilla raised her hand. Corpses stood wavering—some skeletal, some decaying corpses pulled from their rest. She snapped her fingers. And they all wandered off.

The land looked decayed.

Drained.

The kingdoms faded to grey.

"Like I said," the man repeated, "this has *everything* to do with you."

He snapped his fingers. The world collapsed. The Darkness returned. I didn't realize how comforting it would be. Another door opened. I walked through without being told otherwise.

Chairs lined the wall.

Second to last—*Drake*.

I ran and hugged him. He hugged me back in shock.

"What are you doing here??" he asked, confused.

The man said, "He's in line for judgment." As if knowing I'd ask too.

"But he died over a week ago. Why is he still here?" I asked.

The man shrugged, uninterested in our reunion.

I turned back—Drake was gone.

"Drake?" I looked around. *"DRAKE?!"*

The man covered his ears in irritation.

I turned again. Drake was in a guillotine.

I ran, grabbed the latches—but they wouldn't budge.

"NO!"

The blade fell.

Whoooooshing.

Drake's head landed in the basket.

"NOOO!" I shrieked.

I rocked his head in my lap, sobbing.

"TAKE ME INSTEAD!"

The man just watched uncomfortably.

"*WHY ARE YOU JUST STANDING THERE?!*" I screamed.

He pulled out a pocket watch, uneasily then pocketed it again.

"You get a few more minutes. Then you need to pull yourself together. The fate of the world lies with you—and I prefer my existence not to be observing a decayed rock if Camilla gets her way."

I kissed my hand and placed it on Drake's cheek.

Then I stood.

The man nodded softly and led me off.

"You go alone from here." He stated.

"What? Why?" I asked.

"Because my job is done."

He vanished.

I walked forward. A flash of light appeared ahead. I began to sprint. The light surrounded me in a warm embrace almost like a hug.

"OH MY GOD!" a woman's voice echoed. "*HEY! WAKE UP!*"

I kept running.

The light grew brighter.

For a split second, I saw Drake, and my mother, both urging me to escape the afterlife's brutally suffocating grasp.

I groaned as excruciating pain threatened to end me again. I pushed myself up from the floor, gripping my head.

The woman knelt beside me. "Welcome back. I thought we lost you."

"You hungry?" she asked.

I stood. My legs were weak, and wobbly but I managed. I no longer felt empty—just sore.

That was certainly a close call.

Act II: The Threshold Between Then and Never

The woman helped me to my feet and led me into the next room. The decor was elegant—*too elegant*. She sat me at a long table, then returned with a bowl of soup, setting it gently in front of me. I began to sip it, slow and careful; my throat ached with every swallow.

She smiled.

“I’m glad you’re okay,” she said, beaming. “I’m Amelia, but you can call me Amy. What’s your name?”

I took a deep breath between Spoonfuls.

“Akira,” I answered quietly.

Two men entered.

“Hey, you’re awake! That’s great,” said Takka.

Zane sighed. “At least you didn’t die in my bed.”

Amy chuckled.

“So, Akira, where are you from? Do you have family we can find?” she asked.

I shook my head, stood—*dizzy*—and collapsed.

The next thing I knew, I was back in Zane's bed.

"She should rest. It's been a while since she used that much energy," Amy said, sounding more relaxed now.

"I heard King Roldan has ordered a mandatory retreat to Kishak. No reason given—but everyone in the Light Kingdoms is ordered to go," Zane said.

Takka grunted in response, some sound I couldn't decipher.

Zane continued, *"Some of the clergy say King Verath's preparing a siege on Kishak. There's nothing left to stop him. The other kingdoms are abandoned. Khofte won't engage unless provoked. There's even a celebration in Lolem tonight, the posters say '—to help remember those lost to the eclipse, including my dear friend, Drake.' It's said after the memorial he's marking his final push for Rhova."*

A celebration? *Verath is celebrating?* My body began to burn hotter.

I sat up, rage building into a might overwhelming my aches and pains.

"The newspapers say he moves tomorrow," Zane added.

I got out of bed, hobbled unsteadily to the window—and punched it out.

Glass shattered. I climbed through and moved as fast as I could into the woods. My lungs burned, each breath feeling like a bonfire, but at least I was breathing.

"OH MY GOD! AKIRA'S GONE! WE HAVE TO FIND HER!" Amy screamed in the house behind me.

I kept running. The trees opened onto the lake near Ectwë, and I followed the trail toward Sylhalin. It was normally a day-and-a-half walk. I was already a quarter of the way there; Rage was an excellent motivator.

A carriage raced up from behind me; Amy threw the door open.

"Akira! What are you doing?!" she shrieked.

I didn't stop. I had no interest in explaining myself.

Takka spoke without looking away from the road. "If you need a ride, we can help."

I considered it. It *would* get me to Sylhalin quicker. I reached for Amy's hand. She pulled me inside.

She caught her breath. "*So… where* are we going?"

“Sylhalin,” I said firmly.

Takka nodded and the carriage began to pick up speed.

Shortly after, we reached the western gate. Takka slowed as we approached. I climbed out as the guards raised the gate, then hopped back in.

“Where to from *here?*” Takka asked.

I pointed to the observatory on the hill. He turned and led the horses onward.

We pulled up in front. I leapt out. Atlas greeted me at the door with a roar off put by my company it seemed, he rushed and began rubbing his head against mine.

I rubbed his head in return and headed inside.

Amy, Zane, and Takka stared in shock at the tiger.

“Is… is that a *tiger?*” Amy asked.

Atlas bared his fangs with a controlled roar.

“Yes,” I said, heading upstairs, my body shaking from the effort. I gave a whistle, and Atlas padded after me.

I reached the room where I kept my gear—not so much a bedroom, just a cot and dresser. I ditched the tattered gown and pulled on my armor. I wrapped my scarf around my neck, slung my katana across my back, and stepped down the stairs into the foyer.

"*Wow,*" Zane said in awe.

Amy and Takka elbowed him in sync.

I passed them, climbed into the carriage. Atlas took the front steps. I whistled—he leapt into the back.

Zane screamed in surprise.

I urged the horses forward.

As we neared Lolem, the celebration lights glimmered beyond the walls. My mouth tasted of iron as we approached.

I stopped at the gate and dismounted. Amy asked where I was going.

"I'll be back." I said.

I yanked the tower door handle—*locked.* I fired my flintlock. The door flew open.

I charged up the stairs. A soldier waited at the top. I pulled my katana and shoved him back. He growled and resisted. I pushed harder—the blade bit into his chest. He grunted. I drove it through; he fell to the ground and his head hit the floor first.

I reached the top of the tower, ran to the levers, and yanked both. The portcullis began to rise.

I leapt from the tower to a rooftop, then into a hay pile. I adjusted my scarf and slipped into an alley. Takka pulled the carriage inside.

"You guys wait here. I'll be back," I said.

"*Again…?*" Zane whined.

I gave a whistle. Atlas padded beside me as we headed down the street.

The city still bore scars—water damage, shattered windows, scorched banners. We passed a blacksmith's shop. I spotted throwing knives on the counter and strapped them to my belt.

We climbed the stairs toward the palace. Verath was near the top of the sets of decorative steps.

The crowd parted as Atlas, and I approached. Murmurs spread like wildfire.

Atlas bared his fangs. Some people screamed and scattered.

I reached the final step as Verath turned with a smile.

"What a nice surprise," he said. "Come to see me off?"

"Something like that," I said with a scoff.

He turned his back to me to ascend into the palace. I seized my opportunity and threw a knife and watched as—it planted into his calf. He collapsed to the ground.

"*YOU BITCH!*" He bellowed.

His eyes glowed deep red. Spectral warriors appeared around him in the same aggressive aura, readying themself for combat.

I drew my katana, the ring filled the room, I was as ready as I was going to be, I hope they are too.

One lunged—I ducked and slashed. These weren't ghosts. They were enraged echoes.

I fought through them. Verath fled like a coward.

"*Atlas! Find him!*" I ordered, Atlas heeded my call, Atlas charged up the staircase and to the right corridor. I followed, dodging the warriors' attacks.

"*Get off me!*" Verath's voice echoed.

I reached the room at the end of the hall. Verath tried to climb out a window—Atlas had his ankle in his vicelike jaws thrashing wildly.

Verath spun, kicked Atlas through the conjoining window, then as soon as he was free turned and tackled me. Atlas fell to the lower rooftop with an enraged roar. Verath held his focus on me and slammed me into the floor using his weight against me.

He held a dagger to my throat.

"You've ruined *everything*," he spat. "This was supposed to be *legacy. Easy. Clean.*"

His eyes were manic. enraged. The dagger pressed against my skin.

"I am so sick of that disgusting feline. And your FUCKING BOYFRIEND TOO! You know, he actually *BEGGED*. Not for his life—*for yours*, *PATHETIC!*" Verath was seething with manic rage, I thought I might have to shrink to escape from it.

I reached for a knife on my hip and stabbed it into his side. He howled like a wounded animal.

I kicked him off of me and crawled for my katana.

He grabbed my ankle with a firm crack of his fist.

"Oh no you *don't*." He said with a tired laugh. He stabbed his dagger into my lower back. I screamed in agony but continued reaching for my katana.

"You screamed for him. That grief…was the highlight of my life." Verath let out a manic inhale. "Like the smell of blood and sweat after a battle well fought."

I twisted, grabbed my katana, and *sliced*—three of his fingers flew off to the side.

He shrieked and gripped his bleeding hand for a second, swapping it and grabbing a handful of my hair, he cut a chunk off, then slammed my head into the floor with his steadfast grip.

He pummeled me. I tried to fight back. I landed a hit to his jaw, which stunned him and took my chance to run. Verath growled in fury and bolted after me.

He tackled me again, and forcibly rolled me to my back, and drove a blade into my stomach.

I wailed in pain once more. Blood pounded in my ears. Verath's psychotic ramblings came through fragments.

I desperately stabbed his left side, dragging the blade across, His insides sliding outward touching the open air.

He let out a loud scream and rolled off of me and groaned quieter and quieter as he lay nearby. His form took on an ethereal red shimmer as if he were magically steaming.

One last entity formed to his defense—*Drake*.

My heart stopped. The hair on my neck stood watching Drake stand, ready to defend this *monster.*

The ghost spun his staff. but he didn't seem to see me. No recognition of the times we shared. A shell of himself. Which maybe the mercy I deserve right now.

I laid my head flat and stared at the decorative ceiling—a beautiful painting of the landscape between here and Sylhalin, Calís. It was breathtaking. The sun on the crest of the horizon drowned the fields of flowers in a golden glow. A warm puddle of blood emerged around me, dampening my armor and sticking to my bare arms.

Worth it. I inhaled deeply.

I closed my eyes weakly.

"What the hell did you do!?" asked the man in white, his anger with me was bristling into the nearby air.

"You were supposed to preserve the world. Killing Verath changes nothing!"

"I didn't know," I said weakly.

"I can't save you again," he said with an anxious sigh.

He vanished.

"Akira?!" a woman shrieked.

Amy's voice.

"TAKKA! OVER HERE!"

Footsteps clobbered into the room.

"Oh God—what happened?!" Amy sobbed.

"We have to move her!" she screeched.

Everything went quiet.
And that was all that remained.

Silence.

Act III: What I Never Became

"Akira?!" a woman shrieked.

"TAKKA! OVER HERE!"

Footsteps. So many footsteps.

"Oh God—what happened?!" A woman sobbed.

"We have to move her!" she screeched.

The screams proceeded *past me. Instead of me*.

The world was *too loud*. But I'd already stepped away from it, so it didn't matter.

Despite the volcanic eruption of emotion in the room, my senses dulled to a roar in my ears, a man approached the edges of my vision.
"What do you dream of Verath? What was this all for?" The man draped in an exquisite white coat with eyes as soulful blue as the cushioning waves of the sea, knelt beside me.

"Peace." I murmured weakly, struggling to keep my eyes open.

I *know*. *Me*, of *all* people.

But not the kind you sing about in lullabies. Not the *pretty* kind.

I daydream about a room.

Stone walls. A desk. Maybe a window, if the world's feeling kind.

And *silence.*

No screams. No plans. No gods to answer to.

Just the soft sound of a quill on paper. Maybe the rustle of a page turning.
Maybe—*maybe*—someone's breathing, quiet beside me. Not afraid. Not angry. Just… *there*.

In those dreams, I'm not a warlord. Not a king. Not even Verath. I'm a creator, an inventor, a tinkerer.

I'm just a man who never had to build an empire from the wreckage of who he used to be. Not being propelled to meet someone else's image for me.

I daydream about not needing to be anything more than that.
And in those rare moments…
I almost believe I *could've* been.

"I dreamed of peace." I said with a heavy flutter to my eyes, the man nodded intently. Almost sympathetically. "You'll have that soon." He said, his hand moved gently to my eyes and forced them closed. The last of my energy, spent on a shudder through my body.

A meaningful moment of *warmth.*

Connection.

And all that remained of me, as a tear curled down my cheek leaving a cooling trail on my face.

Was *Peace.*

Epilogue

Act I: A Moment Preserved, forever.

They arrived at the gates of Sylhalin under moonlight, the city still quiet, recovering from wounds not yet scarred.

Akira lay limp in the back of the carriage, her breathing shallow. Amy knelt beside her, brushing hair from her blood-crusted forehead.

“She’s burning up,” she whispered. “We have to move fast.”

The guards let them through without a word. They recognized the tiger.

Atlas trotted alongside the carriage, flank streaked with ash and blood, his expression unreadable. His gaze never left Akira.

“I’ll *never* get used to that thing,” Zane muttered, eyeing Atlas with genuine fear. “He looks at me like I’m snack sized.”

Takka grunted. “Just don’t try to pet him.”

“No plans to,” Zane shot back, voice rising half an octave. “I like my limbs right where they are.”

They pulled into the observatory courtyard. The building loomed above them, battered but still standing. Zane jumped down and opened the carriage door. Amy and Takka carefully lifted Akira out, her scarf still damp with blood.

Inside the observatory, everything smelled like dried herbs and gunpowder. Amy guided them to the same room they'd been in before—cot, dresser, quiet corner. It felt distant now. Smaller. Like it had lost its purpose the moment she'd walked away from it.

They laid her gently on the cot. Amy sat at her side, holding her hand. "Come on, Akira. Stay with us."

Takka took a seat by the window. Zane, restless as *always*, paced.

Then he noticed her pack—half open, tucked near the bedpost. Something poked out from a folded journal. Zane crouched, *curious*.

"Hey," he said. "She kept drawings?"

Amy glanced over. "What?"

He carefully tugged it out—a charcoal sketch, smudged from wear. It was a portrait. A man's face. Sharp cheekbones, tousled curls, tired eyes that still managed a crooked smile, illuminated by a small bubble of flame amongst the overwhelming darkness, a sleeping tiger between two figures.

Zane whistled low. “Damn.”

Takka leaned over. “What is it?”

Zane held up the drawing like a lost page from a history book. “I don’t know who this guy was—but Akira drew him like he held the stars together.”

Amy took it gently, her eyes softening. “*Maybe* he did.”

“He’s hot too,” Zane added, unapologetically. “In a rugged, probably emotionally unavailable way. She has taste.”

Amy rolled her eyes. “*Zane*.”

“*What?* I’m just saying! I call ‘em like I see ‘em. You think I don’t notice when people are carved out of marble and pain?”

Takka chuckled. “Carved out of pain?”

“—*And Marble*. But You know she liked him. Look at the jawline. That’s a *love* sketch.”

They laughed—quietly, gently. Not because it was funny, but because love needed a place to breathe.

Amy folded the drawing carefully and returned it to Akira's pack.

"I hope she wakes up," she said. "So, we can ask her who he was."

Zane stood up. "Yeah. Me too. 'Lotta stories left untold."

They settled into the night, each in their own corner of quiet. Atlas lay at the foot of the bed, watching her sleep like he might keep her heart beating just by staying close.

Outside, the wind shifted toward Kishak.

And inside, the war paused—if only for a moment.

Act II: Illuminated by their story.

The observatory had grown quiet, lit only by the soft lantern light hanging near the windows. The rain pounded against the walls like an angry mob. Amy had tucked the sketch carefully back into Akira's pack. Takka stood at the far wall, arms crossed, deep in thought. Zane, still processing, sat on the edge of a table like it offended him with its sturdiness.

"She *really* drew him like that?" he muttered, shaking his head. "I know I said it before but—I stand by it. That man is *hot*. Like, *dangerously* so, they're unnecessarily attractive as a couple."

Amy snorted, half-laughing, half-choking. "*Zane—*"

"I'm just saying! The bone structure? The shoulders? If this sketch is even 80% accurate, Akira's type is… *devastating*."

Takka ignored them both, crouching near Akira's gear again. "There's something else."

"I still don't get why she did it," Takka murmured, staring into the flames. "Verath was a *monster*. A pissed-off, magic-wielding king with a god complex—""-and enough ego to drown a dragon." Amy chimed in.

"So, she gutted him," Amy added softly, polishing her boots.

"She nearly died doing it," Takka added, holding a pot of something steaming. "She did die. Briefly. She still could for all we know."

A long silence followed. The fire popped again.

Then Amy leaned over and dug into the small pack they'd found tucked by the cot when they first carried her into the observatory. "Wait—there's something else. Look."

She pulled out a folded parchment, its edge singed, the ink faded slightly but still smelled fresh. She passed it to Takka first, who read it with furrowed brows before silently handing it to Zane.

Zane blinked. His voice cracked slightly as he read it aloud.

—Akira,

You're asleep beside me right now. The world outside this room is falling apart, but here, it's quiet. You're quiet. And for the first time in my life, I don't want to be anywhere else.

I don't know how I got this lucky.

When I close my eyes, I see it—our little cottage by the waves, your boots by the door, the sound of your laugh echoing in the kitchen, firelight on your face. I see a future, Akira. I see *you.* And gods, I never used to believe in that.

But you made me believe in something worth building.

I know it won't be easy. I know peace is a luxury the world keeps trying to burn. But every dream I've ever had feels small now, compared to the life I want with you. The world can keep tearing itself apart. I just want to hold the pieces that matter.

You.

Your laugh.

The sound of your charcoal scratching paper when you think no one's listening.

The way you look at broken things like they still deserve saving.

I want to see where your story goes. *Our* story goes. I want to be the man who walks beside you—through storms, through quiet, through whatever's left when the smoke clears. I want to build something real, something lasting, even if it's just *one* safe place in a burning world.

I don't care if the future is *war* or *ruin* or *rain*. If you're in it—then it's worth it.

This letter isn't a goodbye.

It's the beginning.

A promise.

A million dreams of us, and every one of them ends with you. I hope, after the fog clears, you think of me not as the talkative man you found in Ectwë, not as the phoenix, Verath captured, but as the boy, whose hand you touched and made him feel whole again.

I love you, Akira.

Always yours, Drake

Silence fell again.

Amy wiped her face before tears could fall.

Takka exhaled slowly and glanced at the window, then toward Akira's still form in the next room.

"He really loved her," Amy whispered.

"She still loves him," Takka replied.

"I'd kill for someone to write me a letter like that," Zane muttered. "That man wrote poetry while she slept, that's *so* sweet."

Zane reached for the lute leaning against the wall. "He wrote his goodbye with love. She fought with it. Maybe we can keep a piece of that."

Takka nodded.

Zane gave a half-smile. "We turning this into a ballad or what?"

They gathered near the window. Zane began to pluck the strings gently, a soft melody echoing through the stone walls. Takka started humming low under his breath, and Amy—voice raw but true—offered words to match the moment.

"The Ballad of a Tigress' Vigil"

Are you lost beneath the moonlight's breath?
Did you wade through fire? Did you dance with death?
Did you hold your ground when the world gave in—
For the ones you love, for the might-have-beens?

Did you cry for peace with a sword in hand?
Bury him deep in the broken land?
Did you scream loud to the sky above,
For the man you killed? For the one you loved?

He wrote your name like a vow in stone,
Loved you loud but died unknown.
And the stars, they wept where the banners fell— The
place where the Tigress roared.
In a war no god would dare to tell.

Oh, will you sing when the crows still call?
Will you rise again if the towers fall?
Will you light the flame when the rot runs deep,
For the ones who wake and the ones who sleep?

(echoed)
For the ones who wake… and the ones who sleep…

Two weeks had passed since Akira brought an end to Verath's reign over the northern regions of Rhova—but the victory came with a price. Akira fell into a two-week coma due to the extent of her injuries. Her newfound colleagues fought to revive her, but to no avail. Camilla's coronation lay only a day away, and with Akira in her state, the trio didn't know they were battling a clock.

Camilla rose to power over Rhova, her powers considered limitless. But hope still remains—Verath's powers lie dormant within someone *new*. Rhova stands on a cliff of despair as Camilla reforms the world in her own image, bringing it to the brink of destruction. Though she cannot physically leave the kingdom of Kishak due to the blessed walls of Rhín…

The walls hold her at bay, but they won't hold forever. For now, Rhova is under her army's control, enslaving those who remain.

Although Camilla holds the continent in her grasp, a coup is forming—right under her nose. All they lack is a *leader*. Verath's war may have ended, but it was not in vain. Akira *will* rise to take her predecessor's place, but will she bring peace to the world again? fulfilling a prophecy once told by the gods. She will explore the roots of her newly obtained abilities while trying to accept the pain of her past.

Four years have passed.

Camilla's rule of terror has left history with one name for this age: *The Time When Hell Walked the Earth.*

Few still hold hope.

The rest have already given up.

The war *will* continue—but *when?*

Epilogue: The Years That Followed

"Mommy, look!" Emily yelled, giggling and clapping. "Look! MONKEY!"

She was pointing—at a lemur. I smiled, picked her up, and pointed to the creature.
"That's a lemur, not a monkey. *Well*, maybe the monkey's cousin."

She covered her face and giggled. The lemur chittered and leapt to a rooftop. Emily wriggled out of my arms, so I set her down and let her run ahead. She sat at the cliffside, watching waves crash into the rocks below, and let out a sigh of relief.

I sat beside her, slower than she had, and joined her gaze at the eastern horizon.

Dendrin walked up behind us, resting a hand on my shoulder.
"Back already?" he asked with a genuine smile.

He ruffled Emily's hair. She grinned at him and turned back to the sunset.

"She's always interested in the past," I said. "Instead of fairy tales, she wants to hear how life in the village *really* was."

He helped me to my feet and led us back to the guest house. He poured tea, and we sat on the porch.

Eventually, Emily began whispering to herself.

"What's she saying?" Dendrin asked, sipping his tea.

"She's talking to her grandmother… *or* her father. This is where she feels most at home."
I smiled. "I can't say I blame her. I share that comfort." Part of me liked that Emily enjoyed being here, some called it morbid, but I knew she meant well.

Dendrin looked at Emily with a warm expression, he reached beside his chair and handed me a small clay pot with a dandelion blooming from the soil. I let out a light gasp.

"*Akira*—here. I know they're your favorite. Every time I see one grow I fight the urge to pot it for you, and I know I say it every time you visit, but… you have a beautiful child. And I'm glad she has something—*anything*—akin to prayer to help her cope, before you know it, I'll be out of a job, it's her calling." he said with a heavy chuckle.

"Is it still considered grief if she never met them?" I asked, curiosity leaping beneath my skin.

I examined the small delicate flower, it hadn't bloomed yet, a stubborn weed to some, but to me, dandelions are magical, never completely gone even when the wind blows them away. I looked to Dendrin with thanks, I knew no words were necessary.

He nodded kindly.
"She may not have gone through the loss, but she knows how you cherished them. Your pain is her pain. Children are very receptive. *Believe me*—I've got *four.*"

He gave a deep belly laugh, and I placed my hand on his, "and how are the kids? How's Kassi?" I asked, Kassi was my biggest fan growing up. She followed me around like a little duckling.

"Kassi is great, she asks about you *all the time*, she drives her mother, and I mad with her questions." Dendrin said with a proud sigh, one a father gives when his child is his worst enemy and his pride and joy. We watched the sun disappear for an hour or so before he asked,
"What will you do when the walls fall, and Camilla is no longer contained?"

I shrugged.
"I don't know. I've let go of so much. I don't move around anymore. We just live in our cottage outside Sylhalin. I guess I haven't thought that far ahead, and what if they never fall? They've stood for ages, maybe that Celestial Man didn't know what he was talking about." I gave a deep sigh, I had been pretty open with Dendrin since Verath and I fought a few years ago.

Including my intense meetings with the mysterious man in white.

Dendrin sipped his tea and set his cup down on the table beside us. "*Akira*," He leaned back, eyes fixed on nothing, voice low.

"There are beings older than time. Not gods, not like the ones we curse or pray to. Not like Camilla, not even like you. They were the first breath into the void. Carved from light, bound to law before there were laws to follow."

He paused, searching my face, weighing the cost of saying more. "Only four ever bore six wings. Only one ever watched the world from above—not to *rule* it, but to *warn* it."
He lets out a slow breath.
"If that was him—if that was *Uriel*—then this isn't just a war anymore. It's a *prophecy.* Maybe even *judgment*."

He looked at me finally. And there was a fear there in the lines of his face—not of death, but of the unknown.
"And if he came to you… then the stars are watching too."
"The Four Seraphim who stood at each corner of the divine order—and do not leave their posts lightly.
But if only one—Uriel—has broken the silence. The others may still remain above, either *unable* or *unwilling* to act." Dendrin released an anxious sigh as Emily twirled near us, her shoulder-length black hair shimmering, her

skin pink with a warm tone and golden-brown eyes glowing in the fading sun.

“I’m ready to go, Mommy. *Daddy’s happy,*” she said.

She turned and waited on the path. I looked to Dendrin, our conversation far from done, but knew I couldn’t keep Emily waiting. I hugged Dendrin goodbye and took her hand.

“How do you know Daddy’s happy?” I asked.

She looked up at me with perfect seriousness.
“He *told* me.”

We walked toward the carriage. Three dragons flew overhead, roaring, before disappearing into the mountain peaks. I helped Emily into the carriage.

As we approached our secluded cottage on the outskirts of Sylhalin, the waves greeted the sound of our arrival. Emily happily hopped to the window of the carriage and stared at the landscape; she loved the sight.

Atlas emerged from the house. Emily squealed in delight and climbed onto his back. He strutted like royalty as she clung to him proudly.

I walked the horses to the stables before returning to the house. My eyes caught the glint of my katana above the mantle. I paused. I missed the feel of it—its weight, its swing.

"Akira? That you?"

I turned. Ryan sat at the kitchen table with a book, slipping in a ribbon before closing it.
"Everything went well?"

I rolled my eyes.
"As well as it could. I think she might enjoy it a little *too* much."

"Where are the girls?" I asked.

"Playing with their toys," he said with a light smile.

I stepped to the doorway and watched them play—dolls dancing, marrying, laughing.
I glanced at the ring on my hand. *Drake's ring.*

My reflection shimmered in the diamonds. Emily laughed again. It was *his laugh.*

I turned away, only for Emily to wrap herself around my legs in a tight hug. I knelt and hugged her back. She smiled and ran back into the room.

There was a knock at the door. Amy barged in with a burlap sack.
"*Hello to you too,*" I muttered.

She walked to the kitchen and unloaded apples into a wooden bowl. Then she gave me that look.

"You know you're still supposed to be resting."

"That was *four* years ago, Amy. *I'm fine.*"

"Takka says you'll never be 100%. The sessions help, but what you went through… you can't just walk away from that."

I didn't argue. My scar on my torso still ached sometimes. It was closed and healed, but never fully quiet. Especially when I let myself think about it. Tired of the interrogation,

I stepped out onto the porch and watched the night sky.

The silence began to ring in my ears—then it became a voice. I looked around.

And then he was there.

The man from before.
White trench coat.
Hair dark, eyes shifting hues of blue.

his wings— twitched and fluttered anxiously as stood behind me, still as a statue aside from them.

Uriel.

“The end draws near. The walls are weakening. You don’t have long before all hope is lost.” He said in a worried tone.

He glanced over his shoulder, paranoid.
“Don’t waste time. *There’s not much left.*”

And he vanished.

“*Akira? You alright?*”

Ryan stepped out onto the porch.

For a moment… I saw Drake. Just for a second.

I blinked. And Drake was gone.

“Yeah,” I said softly.
“I’m… fine…”

I fiddled with the ring on my hand, twisting it round and round making my skin burn from the friction.

Amy and Ryan talked in the kitchen, about something or other.

But I didn't hear them.

I was somewhere else.
Somewhere *deeper*.

Spinning that ring.

My mind only having one repeating question.

What the hell is wrong with me?

A Gaze of the Fallen World:

A few definitions of some of the recurring mentions in the book, mostly, **locations**. I feel the people mentioned get explored in fair enough detail, but a few chapters of their stories are mentioned afterwards. :)

The blessed walls of Rhín: A mysterious and ancient magical barrier that surrounds the massive kingdom of Kishak. The walls are known to trap any mystic who enters, preventing them from ever leaving the kingdom. Their power is said to be intrinsically linked to the royal coronations held within Kishak, a fact that intensified the long and desperate search for a true heir like Camilla.

***Calís*:** A calm and serene countryside, known and admired for its beauty, with its fields and sleepy villages often being the subject of artwork in surrounding kingdoms. It is located between Sylhalin and Lolem and suffered damage during the war, but it will recover. It is also the region Akira travels through to bury Drake.

Ciron: One of the two main continents, located to the east, locked in an ancient war with Rhova. It is the kingdom from which Verath was the "Banished King" and where he still holds power.

Ectwë: A cursed forest in the Sarnawenian region that was once a village of mystics known as the "Heart of Magic". The forest is sentient, and its trees can attack intruders. Outsiders are unwelcome; it is said that the forest will "spit out any outsider," and is dangerous for anyone without strong magical resistance. Its air can be thick and suffocating, and the spiritual energy has an "acidic touch" that can harm those unprotected.

Eîthor: The one Dark Pillar, standing in opposition to the five Light Pillars. It is a port kingdom that appears as a "grey crown on the continent's jagged brow" and serves as Verath's stronghold in Rhova. Located in an isolated valley shadowed by "towering cliffsides" and "stone mountain barriers," the kingdom struggles with farmland and survives on fishing and food imported from Ciron.

Khofte: A mountainous kingdom situated on an extinct volcano that towers over the continent. Politically, it is a neutral kingdom that is largely left alone. It is ruled by Count Dendrin, a cleric and Akira's surrogate father figure. The kingdom is known for the dragons and their priests that can be seen soaring through its mountain peaks. Its closest neighbors are the abandoned Castle of Zodan, Rostov's second attempt at rebuilding his rule after the raid of Zodan, he ultimately abandons it and lives in a caravan, the castle is at the base of its mountain, and the kingdom of Eîthor in the valley far below.

Kishak: Known as the largest kingdom in the world, ruled by Lord Roldan. It is entirely surrounded by the "blessed walls of Rhín," a magical barrier that traps any mystic who enters.

Lolem: A beautiful and prosperous kingdom ruled by Queen Cilmair. It is known throughout Rhova as a haven for engineers, scientists, and freethinkers who serve the queen. The city is famed for its advanced architecture, featuring tall buildings, waterfalls, and a palace that glows with magic. Lolem is also the host of the grand Lunar Eclipse Festival.

The Pillars: The collective name for the five Light Kingdoms on the continent of Rhova that stand in opposition to the Dark Pillar of Eîthor. They were conquered by the tyrant Lord Rotik in the Second Age.

Rhova: The western continent where most of the story takes place. It is in a state of constant war with the continent of Ciron, a conflict between the forces of "Light" and "Dark".

Sarnawen: One of the five Light Pillars, ruled in secret by Queen Camilla, the "queen without a face". From a distance, its city lights cast a "golden-based aura among the stars". It is a major military power in Rhova.

Sylhalin: An elven city of great strategic importance, known as the "Gated Kingdom". Its observatory is considered the "eyes of Rhova". The city itself is built of marble with large wooden gates, and it is protected by a massive iron-bar dome that can erupt from the walls. Before its liberation, its elven citizens were tortured and enslaved by Imperial armies, forcing some into an underground resistance.

Zodan: Akira's home village, located within the kingdom of Khofte. It was a coastal village that was raided by

Imperials; during the raid, part of the village sank into the sea. The ruins of the village are overseen by the newly rebuilt towering ***Stronghold of Zodan***, which dendrin has taken residence in. Lord Rostov's former stronghold, around which a small settlement of simple huts has formed, reforming the once prosperous village's image from before the raid.

Dramatis Personae: (The People of Rhova)

Akira: The protagonist. A skilled warrior originally from the village of Zodan in Khofte. After her mother was murdered during an Imperial raid, she was trained as a child soldier before being rescued by Count Dendrin. She later reclaims the city of Sylhalin from Rostov and becomes its reluctant leader.

Camilla (Queen): The secret ruler of Sarnawen, known only as the "queen without a face". She is a full-blooded mystic and the long-lost heiress of the tyrant Lord Rotik. After being crowned, she shatters the moon and begins an age of terror, contained only by the blessed walls of Rhín.

Cilmair (Queen): The ambitious and powerful ruler of the kingdom of Lolem. She forges a strategic alliance with Verath to consolidate her power but is later executed by him in the aftermath of her kingdom's destruction.

Dendrin (Count): The kind, religious lord of the kingdom of Khofte. He led the search for the children of Zodan and rescued Akira, acting as her surrogate father figure and providing her a safe haven.

Drake: A full-blooded mystic with the powers of a phoenix. He was the husband of Theresa and father of Mixa, who he lost during the fall of Ectwë, where he was trapped inside a tree for years. After being freed by Akira, he becomes her closest companion and eventual husband. He is tragically executed by Verath.

Mixa: The six-year-old daughter of Drake and Theresa. She was lost during the destruction of her village, Ectwë.

Roldan (Lord): The ruler of the massive kingdom of Kishak and the appointed Lord over the five Light Pillars.

Rostov (Lord): A cruel and formidable man known for hunting people for sport in the Sarnawenian forest. He captures Drake, takes control of Sylhalin, and renames it New Zodan. He is ultimately killed by Akira, who he names as his successor with his dying words.

Rotik (King): A historical tyrant from the Second Age who conquered and ruled all five Light Pillars. His secret daughter with a mystic from Ectwë was the heiress, Camilla.

Ryan: A loyal guard from Lolem who Akira befriends after the city is flooded. He loses his wife in the disaster but is reunited with his daughter, Clea, and becomes a close friend and ally to Akira.

Sam: A light elf from the Sylhalin resistance who becomes Verath's trusted lieutenant and moral compass. He is inadvertently killed by Akira in Ectwë, an act that solidifies Verath's hatred for her.

Theresa: Drake's wife, a mystic from Ectwë with the power to manipulate water. She wrote a diary detailing the village's final days before she was lost in its destruction.

***Uriel*:** One of the four ancient Seraphim, described as beings "older than time" who guard the "divine order". He appears to Akira as a man in a white trench coat with six wings to warn her that the blessed walls of Rhín are weakening and the end is near.

***Verath*:** The protagonist antagonist, known as the "Banished King of Ciron" and ruler of the Dark Pillar of Eîthor. He is a powerful deathwalker haunted by the ghost of his abusive father. His obsessive quest for power and his hatred for Akira lead him to commit numerous atrocities, including the execution of Drake. He is ultimately killed by Akira.

Scars in the Margins:

This is a collection of excerpts from our main protagonists and focal characters. I'm not giving you all the answers, but a few more than the text may.

The Last Resort:

Drake

The air in Ectwë had grown thin, stretched taut with fear. It had been *weeks* since King Rotik's forces surrounded us, their shadows falling long and hungry over our homes. At night, Theresa would write by candlelight, the quill scratching against parchment the only sound besides our daughter Mixa humming to her worn teddy bear. I'd watch them, a perfect, fragile picture, and feel a cold dread seep into my bones. The village elders had already enforced a curfew; they spoke in hushed, frantic tones of a "last resort" if Rotik's soldiers breached our wards. I had little clue what it entailed, but I suspected it had *everything* to do with his heiress.

Theresa didn't want to go. When the elders mandated that all combat-capable mystics join the scouting mission, she fought them. "*I don't want to leave Mixa,*" she told me, her voice trembling. But they had threatened exile, and we had nowhere else to go. I kissed her goodbye at the edge of the Sarnawenian Forest, her hand lingering in mine before we split off. The last words I saw from her were written in her journal "*I'll find you, Mixa. I promise,*" she had written in her diary before she left, a vow I knew she would die to keep.

Her absence left a void, I knew she planned to desert the elder's militarization and yet, I did little to stop her. A silence that the whispers from the trees couldn't fill. The night she was due to return, the horns blew. Not horns of victory, but of panic. Rotik's forces were breaking through.

The elders gave the order. The Last Resort was upon us.

It was a forbidden rite, a final, merciless defense passed down from our highest deity, Eluriah, the Keeper of Life and Flame. We were to give the forest a *heart*, a *consciousness*, a *rage* to protect what was left of our people. The children were taken first, hurried away to the southern edge of the village for release. I saw Mixa being led away, clutching her bear, her small face a mask of confusion. I wanted to run to her, to *hold* her, but my *duty* was here. I was a full-blooded mystic, a *phoenix*, and my fire was needed for the rite.

We gathered in the village center, the last of the mystics. The ground trembled as we began the incantation. I felt the magic of the earth *surge* up through my feet—*raw*, *ancient*, and *terrifying*. It was the power to manipulate plant life on a massive scale, the very magic that had made the women in the village targets. "*The Heiress! She brings salvation!*" The crowd seemed relieved, until the plants didn't seem to *aid* us in our fight.

The trees around us groaned, their bark *twisting* and *splintering*. I watched in horror as *agonizing* faces began to form in the wood, their silent screams echoing the chaos in my own heart. Roots erupted from the ground, thick as pythons, lashing out at the invading soldiers and mystics alike. This was not the gentle magic of our village; this was a defense born of genocide, an act of ultimate, brutal peace. A little girl's scream filled the air. My instincts snapped to attention. *Mixa.* I whipped towards the sound and searched for her. I saw a girl in the darkness being pulled from a hollow tree by two intruders, I dashed towards them trying to cover as much distance as possible.

My own power surged, flames erupting from my hands, hotter than anything I had ever summoned. But it wasn't controlled. The rite was too powerful, the collective fear and rage of the mystics feeding it until it became a wild, insatiable thing, but something else thrust everything out of proportion.

Through the haze of fire and screaming, I saw her. *Theresa.* She had returned from her mission only to find her home in flames, her people sacrificing themselves. Our eyes met for a fraction of a second. I saw her mouth form my name. She pulled water from the wells and fought off soldiers with whips of water, attempting to put out the infernos claiming her home.

Then the world became fire and wood. The tree beside me swung a branch, and I felt a crushing blow. The magic poured into me, *through* me, and I felt myself being pulled apart. My own screams joined the chorus as my body was drawn into the trunk of the ancient tree, my flesh and bone merging with bark and sap. My last coherent thought was of Mixa's teddy bear, left *alone* on the floor of our empty home. I was no longer a man. I was *rage*. I was *vengeance*. I was a prisoner in a wooden shell, a guardian of a cursed forest that had once been the Heart of Magic, now reduced to nothing but bones under ivy. And all that remained of me was the *waiting.*

A Whisper of Steel and Salt:

Akira

The first thing I remember is the smoke, *thick* and *salty*, burning my lungs. Then came the sound of Imperial boots—a dreadful, rhythmic thunder that crushed the familiar song of the sea. Our door splintered open, and my mother was there, her face a mask of terror and resolve. She shoved her katana into my hands. The steel was cold, heavy, and felt impossibly large in my small grasp.

"*Run, Akira,*" she commanded, her voice a desperate whisper. "*Don't look back. Help who you can.*"

I did as she said. I ran. In an alley, I found a little boy, no older than six, sobbing behind a rain barrel. I grabbed his hand, pulling him along as I tried to find a safer place for us to hide. But we didn't get far. An Imperial soldier stepped out from the shadows, his armor blocking the narrow path. I tried to lift my mother's sword, but it was too heavy. He snatched it from my grasp with a cruel laugh before grabbing both me and the boy.

He threw us into a cramped cage on the back of a wagon with other terrified children from the village. I felt a wave of despair wash over me; I had *failed* my mother, and I had lost her sword.

It was from inside that cage that I saw her last. She burst into the town square, her eyes wild with panic, searching.

Then she saw me. A harrowing scream tore from her throat, a sound of pure anguish that silenced the chaos for a heartbeat. All thoughts of defense vanished; she had only *one* mission. She fought to get to me, a force of nature against a tide of steel. *"MAMA!!"* I thrust myself through the slats of the cage fighting to *get* to her, to *help* her. Only to be rebuffed by the soldier who had captured me.

But she never made it. A man in dark armor met her charge in the center of town. I watched, helpless, as he jammed a sword through her head. I saw her eyes go dark, her jaw fall slack. With a casual shove of his foot, he pushed her body from his blade and let it *fall.*

The world went silent. As the wagons began to move, the soldier who had captured me walked past our cage and tossed the katana inside. It landed with a heavy thud, the metal cold against my skin. At that same moment, the ground began to tremble. I don't know *how* it happened—a *spell,* a *monster*, or the sea's own *rage*—but as we were pulled away, I watched half of my village, my *home*, sink beneath the waves.

The wagon rattled on, carrying us away. I sat in the darkness, surrounded by the quiet sobs of the other children, the immense weight of my mother's sword in my lap. It was no longer a weapon of defiance, but a cold, heavy testament to *everything* I had just *lost*.

The Edge of Vengeance:

Akira

Freedom was a gilded cage. After Count Dendrin and his soldiers freed us from the Imperial barracks, he brought the few surviving children back to his newly rebuilt estate in Khofte. The remaining half of Zodan had begun replacing some of the homes and the businesses that had sunk that fateful day, Lord Rostov had lost interest in his rule after the raid, He began his hunt, Dendrin claimed rule. He was a deeply religious man, his faith a palpable force, but he had not yet become the cleric I would later know him as; he was still a lord accustomed to war and justice. He gave me a room with a soft bed and clean linen, but I slept on the floor by the door. Comfort felt like a weakness I could no longer *afford*. Something I no longer *deserved*.

Dendrin was patient, but he did not understand. He saw a child he had rescued; I saw a soldier who had *failed* her final mission—*protecting my mother*. The other children slowly began to remember how to play. I only remembered how to *fight.*

He found me one night in the stronghold's training yard, going through sword forms with a wooden practice dummy, my mother's katana, a cold, heavy weight in my hands.

"The war is over for you, *Akira*," he said gently, his voice carrying across the silent yard. "You are *safe* here."

I didn't stop my movements. The blade whistled through the air. "It's *not* over," I said, my voice low and tight. I finally turned to face him, the moonlight glinting off the steel. "When I am strong enough, I am going to *hunt* the man who killed my mother. I will make him regret it—make him watch me kill *everyone* he *loves* while he watches from a cage". The thought sated my rage, and I felt my words drip venom.

I saw a deep sadness in Dendrin's eyes. He was a man of God, and he did not believe in vengeance. He and my mother had that in common. "That is a dark path, child," he warned. "It will hollow you out until nothing is left."

"I'm already hollow," I replied. "This is the only thing left to fill the space."

He knew then that he could not stop me. He saw the promise I had made to myself was not one I would ever break. He continued to care for me, but our time together had changed. Our conversations grew shorter, and I realized I had run out of things to say on the matter. He was trying to save a soul, and I was sharpening a weapon.

The day I left, he did not try to dissuade me. He simply gave me a sturdy pack, a full water skin, and a small pouch of gold. "Vengeance will *not* bring her back, Akira," he said as I mounted the horse he had prepared for me. "But I pray you survive long enough to find that out for yourself, Queen Cilmair has a job for a new lead royal guard, I think it would be something you could consider." He placed a concerned hand on my shoulder. "You will always have a home here, should you choose to return." I nodded, unable to speak past the lump in my throat. I was grateful for his kindness, but I could not accept it. *Not yet.* I rode away from Khofte not as a rescued child, but as a hunter. My mother's katana was on my back, and the face of her killer was burned into my mind. I had a new war to fight.

The Perfect Prey:

Rostov

The Sarnawenian Forest offers the only sport worthy of a man of my station. *The hunt* is an art, a conversation between *predator* and *prey*, and I am its *greatest* artist. I had released the tigress from her comfy cage with her whimpering cub the evening before, giving her just enough time to reclaim her wildness before our game began. I was almost torn between her and the Mystic I had claimed, but his *incessant* babbling about his savior, *Akira.* Left a bad taste in my mouth, his tears would soil my victory. *Not much of a hunt.* Tigers on the other hand, are a *rarity*, almost extinct, and this one was a *magnificent* specimen—*powerful*, *intelligent*, a *true* challenge.

I found her tracks by a stream, the prints deep in the mud. But they were not alone. *Four*, no, *five* sets of shoddy boot prints mingled with hers. *Refugees*, perhaps? Fleeing the recent skirmishes. How *sloppy*. They would ruin the purity of the hunt. My initial irritation, however, soon gave way to a more delightful thought. Why settle for *one* prize when the forest offered *six*? The beast would be the main event, of course. The humans would be the *appetizer*.

They were *clumsy*, leaving a trail a blind man could follow. I stalked them for an hour, savoring the rising panic in their hushed whispers. They knew they were being followed. They could feel the forest watching them.

I cornered them in a small clearing against a rockslide. There was no escape. The tigress, sensing the trap, let out a low growl, her body tensing as she placed herself between me and the pathetic humans. A protector. How wonderfully ironic.

“Good evening!” I called out, stepping from the trees. “A beautiful night for a run, isn’t it?”

Their faces were a delicious canvas of *terror*. I explained the rules simply: they had a *ten-minute* head start. The tigress, *however*, was *mine* to claim whenever I *wished*.

The game was brief, and honestly, *disappointing*. They scattered like panicked birds. Beginning their useless squawking. I picked them off one by one with my flintlock, each shot a testament to my skill. They were merely *obstacles*, a way to pass the time before the true sport truly began.

Finally, only the tigress remained. She was *everything* I had hoped for—a whirlwind of *fang* and *claw*. She was *fast*, driving me back with a ferocity that made my blood *sing*. Her claws tore through my coat, leaving a deep wonderful gash across my chest, the warm sting of it only heightening my *excitement.*

But in the end, skill *always* triumphs over instinct. I dodged a lunge, my own blade finding its mark in her side. She fell with a final, defiant roar. I stood over her, breathing heavily, my heart pounding with the thrill of victory. This was *true* power. This was what it meant to be alive. I knelt, admiring the fine quality of her pelt. A shame to have to kill such a *beautiful* creature, but a hunt without a trophy is merely a stroll through the woods. I looked back in the direction of my camp, where a far more interesting prize now awaited. "A fine warm-up," I mused, wiping the blood from my blade. *"Now for the mystic."*

Softness Was Death:

Verath

Before I was a king, I was a collector of secrets. My greatest secret was a small, three-legged fox I'd found in the woods bordering the Ciron palace grounds. Her leg had been caught in a hunter's trap, and I'd spent weeks secretly tending to the wound, sneaking her scraps from the kitchen. I was meant to be at sword practice with my brothers, but I'd slipped away. I was never much of a soldier anyway; my heart was in alchemy, and magic alike, anything *magnificent*. In the quiet study of how things healed and grew. The fox was the closest I'd ever come to putting that passion into practice.

She was finally trusting me enough to eat from my hand. I had nicknamed her *cheaddar,* after her favorite cheese, and the unique shade of orange in her coat, when a *shadow* fell over us.

"*So, this is where the king's youngest son hides.*"

My father's voice was like a grinding stone. He stood tall, his armor immaculate, his face a mask of *disappointment*. I scrambled to my feet, trying to hide the fox behind my legs, but it was too late. He had already seen her. He had seen my weakness.

"What is that?" he asked, his voice *dangerously* calm.

“Nothing, Father. Just a stray.”

“It is a *broken* thing. *Useless*,” he said, his eyes cold as he drew the ornate dagger from his belt. He didn't move toward Cheddar, however. He moved toward me. "I have told you, *Verath.* Weakness is *shame*. Silence is *failure.* Softness is *death*".

He crouched, grabbing cheddar with one hand and holding the dagger to her throat with the other. The small creature gave a terrified whimper, pressing against my leg for protection. I clenched my fists together as I backed away from him on all fours, tears welled in my eyes, it was my fault that this poor defenseless creature was in this situation.

"You will not be an *alchemist*," he growled. "You will *enlist*. Like your *brothers*! *Now*, you will learn the cost of your softness".

My heart hammered against my ribs. I thought he was going to kill her. But his plan was *crueler*.

"You will turn your back on this *pathetic* creature," he commanded, his voice a low thunder. "You will walk back to the palace and not look back. *Prove* to me that you can abandon a weakness when ordered. If you *hesitate*, if you so much as *glance* over your shoulder, I will *end* its life. The choice is *yours*."

Tears crept down my cheeks, but I knew better than to let them all fall. *To be vulnerable is to be weak.* I looked from the dagger at Cheddar's throat to my father's unyielding face. To *save* her, I had to *betray* her.

It was the *hardest* thing I have ever done. I stood up, turned my back on the little life I had *fought* to save, and walked away. Every step was an agony. I could feel the Cheddar's terrified eyes on my back. I didn't look back. I didn't dare. I just walked, the sound of my own footsteps drowning out the *frantic* beating of my heart.

My father followed a few paces behind. As we cleared the woods, he placed a heavy hand on my shoulder. It wasn't a gesture of comfort. It was a brand.

"Good," was all he said.

I didn't save the Cheddar that day. I only saved her from my father's blade. I learned his lesson well: to care for something was to give him a weapon to use against me. And that was the day I began to build my walls; the day I started to bury the soft part of myself. It was the first time I understood that *sometimes, the only way to protect something is to pretend you don't love it at all.*

The Sea-Worn Tomb:

Verath

During the First Age, *long* before my banishment, my father would drag my brothers and I to Eîthor, to teach us the "*family secrets*" to ruling an empire. I was one of five princes of Ciron, but I was the one who learned to live in the shadows. While my brothers practiced swordplay in the castle courtyard, I would steal away to the docks, my heart set on a different kind of power—one my father would have called an *abomination*. My master resided in a place known only to a few: a sea-worn tomb deep beneath the foundations of Sylhalin, its only entrance a hidden sea cave under the cliffs of Lolem .

I would sail there under the cover of night, the salt spray a welcome mask for the fear and exhilaration that churned within me. The cave was a place of forgotten whispers, the air thick with the dust of ages. It was there he taught me the *art of the deathwalker*.

"It is *not* a gift," he warned me during one of our first lessons, his voice a dry rasp. "It is a *debt.* Every time you reach across the veil, you pay a price."

I didn't care. *Any* price was worth escaping the future my father had planned for me, a life where I was just a *pale imitation* of my brothers. I would not be *just* a soldier. I would be *better*.

Inside a chamber of ancient sarcophagi, he commanded me to begin. "Focus," he instructed. "Do not think of the soldier he was. Think of the *echo* he left behind. Become the vessel."

I closed my eyes, reaching out with a will forged in defiance. I pushed past the silence and felt it—a flicker of cold, a wisp of sorrow. The moment I connected, a torrent of memories—*not my own*—crashed into my mind: the shock of a mortal wound, the fading light, the regret of a life cut short. I staggered back, the phantom pain stealing my breath.

"You are a *conduit*, not a *passenger!*" my master's voice snapped, pulling me from the abyss. "*Control it!*"

I grit my teeth, using the anger I felt toward my father as an anchor. With a surge of will, I pulled. A purple orb of energy pulsed in the air, and from the sarcophagus, a translucent spirit in a hollow green aura rose, its *empty* eyes fixed on me. I had done it. This power was *mine*.

But as the spirit bowed, a deep, invasive cold rushed into my bones, a *chill* that no fire could warm. My master saw the triumphant sneer on my face and his expression hardened.

"You see them as *weapons* for your future wars," he said, his tone sharp with disappointment. "You are *wrong*." He stepped closer, his gaze pinning me in place.

"Remember this, Verath," he warned, his voice low and severe. *"Abuse of your connection with the spirits will only drive you to madness. If the spirits use you as a conduit too often, you'll lose yourself to them, forever.* He told me that the cold I felt was the *price—a fragment of death* that would now live inside me. I sailed back to Eîthor that night, the cold a permanent scar on my soul. I knew this *forbidden* magic would one day be the cause of my exile, but in the dark of my cabin, I smiled. I had found the power to become the man my father could *never* control.

What the Roots Remember:

Camilla

Long before I was a queen, I was a child who *loved* the feel of dirt beneath her fingernails. In Ectwë, the Heart of Magic, the soil *hummed* with life, and I could feel it all. Mother said I *shared* her gift, the ability to *coax* life from the ground.

The night it ended, I was tending to my patch of night-blossoms when the screaming started. Mother burst from our cottage, her face *pale* with terror. She didn't grab a weapon; she grabbed *me*.

"Run, my little bloom," she whispered, shoving me toward the thickest part of the woods. "*Run and do not look back. Do not let them see you."*

I did as she said. I *ran*. But I looked back once. I saw the armored soldiers, their swords glinting in the firelight, smash through our door. That was the last time I ever saw my home.

The forest was chaos. I was *small*, and the sounds of battle were everywhere. I hid in the hollow of a great oak, my heart hammering against my ribs. I stayed there for what felt like an *eternity*, until the shouting grew *closer*. Two Imperial soldiers found my hiding spot.

"Look what we have here," one of them sneered, his eyes cold. "A little mystic *rat*."

They cornered me against the ancient tree, their swords drawn. There was nowhere left to run. I was *terrified,* and the world seemed to shrink to the points of their blades. I *squeezed* my eyes shut and pressed my hands to the damp earth, bracing for the end. *"MIXA!?"* I heard a man yell.

But the end *didn't* come. Instead, I felt a familiar hum surge up from the ground, a *wild*, *angry* power that answered the *terror* in my heart. It was my magic, but it felt *different*—not the *gentle* coaxing of a flower, but a *violent,* primal scream.

The ground beneath the soldiers erupted.

Thorny vines, thick as my arm, burst from the soil, wrapping around their legs and armor. Nearby trees' bark splintered and split to reveal faces of fury and fear, rushing to my defense. "*The Heiress! She brings salvation!"* Echoed above the combat and furious trees. The imperial soldiers shouted in surprise, then in pain, as the thorns dug into their steel and flesh. Pale, ghost-like flowers—the kind Mother warned me never to touch—bloomed in an instant around them, releasing a *shimmering* pollen. The soldiers began to gasp and claw at their own faces, screaming at horrors only they could see.

I didn't watch them die. I opened my eyes, saw the *monstrous* garden my fear had created, the sounds of combat had ceased, and my people were gone, replaced by trees where they stood. *My home*. *My mother*. and I turned and kept running. The scar from that night wasn't just the loss of my mother and my home; it was the *terrifying* knowledge of what my own power could do when I was *scared* enough to use it.

What Remains in the End

A final note from the author.

Dear reader,

If you made it this far — *Thank You. Truly. :)*

You stayed through the violence, the silence, the sorrow.

You stayed when it got hard, when it got heavy.

When the grief stopped being literary and started feeling personal.

That means a lot to me.

This wasn't written to be clean. It wasn't plotted with precision or polished for praise. It's been read so many times I know it by heart, but I also lived it.

It was written because I needed something to hold onto when everything else felt like it was slipping away. I shared the earliest versions with my dad. He was my

earliest proof "listener" because most of the book wasn't written to this extent. It was nothing more than an *idea* then, I forced so much of my grief into this book because part of me was truly fighting to get through the loss. *It was survival in story form — blood turned into ink.*

I didn't expect it to reach anyone. Only one person truly mattered in my mind when I started this journey. *My Dad.* He was a pain in my ass, but he was one of my *favorite* people, and though we weren't terribly close for a few years, I cherish the time I *did* have with him towards the end,

But if it reached you — if you saw yourself in Akira's rage, in Drake's quiet hope, in Verath's self-destruction— or you sensed something in the imaginary tear splotches I left in the margins.

then *maybe* it was worth all the breaking it took to get here.

Some people will say it's too raw. Too much. Too messy.

But so is the grief I felt and bled into this.

So is the love I fought so hard to preserve — even when it felt like it would evaporate in the heat of my own rage.

So is the effort I left behind trying to live with both in tandem.

There are pieces of me scattered across these pages — in every death, every choice, every word left unsaid.

And now, *maybe*, there are pieces of you here too.

Caught in the cracks. In the pauses. In the wounds we didn't bandage.

This isn’t closure. It’s not a full stop.

But it is the end of the emptiness.

Because what remains in the end isn’t *perfection.*

It’s not a happy ending or a clear answer.

It’s the people we carry. The scars we keep.

The ones who made us feel *something* — even if it *hurt* losing them.

So, thank you. For holding this story.

For feeling it. For surviving it.

Whatever you carry from here — I hope it matters. I’ll carry it too. It’s the least I can do.

I hope this made you feel less alone.

With all my heart,

Your friend,

Tony :p

P.S. If it hurts — *good.* That means your heart still works. :)

And I’m very proud that you read some of my most vulnerable thoughts and didn't run.

At the beginning of this journey, when my world was *excruciating. Sad. Exhausting.*

And now :) when I'm *okay.*

You're *okay.*

And you didn't shut it down just because I forgot a period or leaned too hard on comma splices. The beginning of this, my *start* to this, may have come off as petulant, disregarding literary rules, but actually, I was a whirlwind, of sadness, anger, fear, I was fighting to have something. *Anything.* That reminded me wholeheartedly of my dad. of how I felt disoriented, like I was forgetting his face, his laugh, and the good times we shared. I was just disregarding rules that suffocated and diminished the work, most genres weren't built for this, so I tried to make it fit, but you know what?

Together, we saw that death *isn't* the end.

It's merely an *interlude* —

Between reuniting with your loved one again *someday and* learning to live without them. *Somehow.*

The end. :) I hope to see you for book 2! *The Resonance of Heresy!*

Anthony J Haight

www.ingramcontent.com/pod-product-compliance
Lightning Source LLC
Chambersburg PA
CBHW020945310726
48980CB00001B/66
9798999121820